"Success, American-style . . . A modern morality tale—curt, clear, concise, and painfully relevant."

—*Saturday Review*

"A powerful and affecting vision of what it is like for some people to live in America today."

—*Publishers Weekly*

"No native-born American could have de͜͡l͜ ͜ ͜ ͜ e themes in quite this way; here t͜ ͜ ͜ the 'inside', very kn͜

"One of the foremo͜ ͜ ͜ world."

—*Psychology Today*

"Relentless talent. Kosinski's work glistens with social observation and psychological apprehension."

—*Time*

"Reading Kosinski is like swimming in a placid sea and suddenly being caught in an undertow."

—*National Observer*

"Flawless . . . A strong meaningful voice, adding something vital to the riches of the modern novel."

—*The Times*, London

Also in Arrow by Jerzy Kosinski

PASSION PLAY
PAINTED BIRD
COCKPIT

THE DEVIL TREE

JERZY KOSINSKI

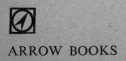

ARROW BOOKS

Arrow Books Limited
17–21 Conway Street, London W1P 5HL

An imprint of the Hutchinson Publishing Group

London Melbourne Sydney Auckland
Johannesburg and agencies
throughout the world

This revised and expanded edition first published
in Great Britain 1982

ACKNOWLEDGMENTS
Lines from "Crazy Jane Talks with the Bishop" from
Collected Poems by William Butler Yeats: copyright 1933 by
Macmillan Publishing Co., Inc., © 1961 by Bertha Georgie
Yeats. By permission of Macmillan Publishing Co., Inc.,
Macmillan London Ltd., M. B. Yeats, and Anne Yeats.
Lines from "Shine, Perishing Republic" from The Selected
Poetry of Robinson Jeffers by Robinson Jeffers: copyright
1925, 1953 by Robinson Jeffers. Lines from "To His Father"
from The Selected Poetry of Robinson Jeffers by Robinson
Jeffers: copyright 1924, 1952 by Robinson Jeffers. By
permission of Random House, Inc.
Lines from "Dear Judas" from Dear Judas and Other Poems
by Robinson Jeffers: copyright 1929 by R. Jeffers, © 1957 by
Robinson Jeffers, © 1977 by Liveright Publishing Corporation.
By permission of Liveright Publishing Corporation.
Lines from The Perennial Philosophy by Aldous Huxley:
copyright © 1944, 1945 by Aldous Huxley. By permission of
Harper & Row, Inc.
Quotations by Heschel, from Abraham J. Heschel's Who Is
Man? published by Stanford University Press.

Set in Times

Made and printed in Great Britain
by The Anchor Press Ltd
Tiptree, Essex

ISBN 0 09 927520 1

AUTHOR'S NOTE

When I wrote this novel initially, I felt restricted by the proximity of its story to the environment and events of my recent past decade. This might account for the cryptic tone of the novel's first version.

Now, years later, in this revised and expanded edition, I have felt free to reinstate all the additional links that bound Jonathan James Whalen to those whom he loved.

JERZY KOSINSKI

To Katherina
and to the memory of my mother

Beyond all agony and anxiety lies the most important ingredient of self-reflection: the preciousness of my own existence. To my own heart my existence is unique, unprecedented, priceless, exceedingly precious, and I resist the thought of gambling away its meaning.

ABRAHAM JOSHUA HESCHEL,
Who Is Man?

The native calls the baobab "the devil tree" because he claims that the devil once got tangled in its branches and punished the tree by reversing it. To the native, the roots are branches now, and the branches are roots. To ensure that there would be no more baobabs, the devil destroyed all the young ones. And that's why, the native says, there are only full-grown baobab trees left.

JERZY KOSINSKI,
The Devil Tree

Looking down at the river shimmering in the bright sun, Jonathan Whalen leaned against the steel balustrade at the end of the street. The skyline of New York that he remembered did not seem altered by the recent skyscrapers. Far across the river, jets took off from La Guardia, leaving behind them thin lines of exhaust. On the near side, a helicopter lifted into the sky, hovered over the water, then veered off, casting its shadow on the river. Another helicopter descended and touched down, quivering to a stop on the landing pad.

Whalen walked toward the heliport, where a freshly painted copter sat on a platform. A large sign proclaimed: EXECUTIVE HELIWAYS, INC. SEE MANHATTAN FROM THE AIR. LOW-RATE EXCURSIONS. Whalen went into the ticket office, and the clerk looked him up and down.

"I'd like to see Manhattan," said Whalen.

"Why don't you take a subway?" said the clerk, focusing on Whalen's old shirt, worn pants, and scuffed boots.

"Manhattan can't be seen from the subway."

"How about the bus?"

"Too slow. How about the sight-seeing flight?"

The clerk leaned across the counter. "Look, this is Executive Heliways, not freeload ways. Understand?"

"I do," said Whalen. He held out several crisp bills, the exact amount listed on the wall board as the price for the half-hour flight. "Will this do?"

Shuffling uneasily, the clerk stared at the money. "I'll check with the pilot," he mumbled as he disappeared into the back room, and a moment later he returned, accompanied by a man in a gray uniform.

"This is the fella who wants to take the ride," said the clerk.

The pilot glanced at Whalen. "Look, son—"

"I'm not your son," said Whalen, and he pushed the money toward the clerk.

The pilot hesitated. "I'm going to have to sort of frisk you before takeoff."

"You frisk everyone who flies with you?"

"Well—at my discretion."

"Then use it," said Whalen.

"It's easier if you put your hands up," said the pilot, approaching him slowly, and as Whalen complied, the man rapidly patted his shirt and pants. "Take off your boots," he directed. Again Whalen obeyed, then put them back on after the inspection. Reassured, the pilot snapped, "Let's board," and the two of them marched toward the landing platform.

Inside the helicopter the pilot turned to Whalen. "We'll fly all over the place," he said; "over the Harlem black, the Gramercy Park white, and the Chinatown yellow; over the Bowery poor and the Park Avenue rich; the East Side, the West Side, midtown, downtown." He pulled the throttle. The machine coughed, vibrated, and arched off the ground.

"A helicopter makes me feel free," said Whalen as he glanced at the tourists watching them through binoculars from the roof of the Empire State Building. "Still, each time I fly in one, I feel like a toy, guided by remote control by someone on the ground."

They passed over the town houses of Greenwich Village. "Now I'll show you where all the big money is," said the pilot, spinning the helicopter toward the Stock Exchange.

"Could you slow down over that building for a second?" asked Whalen. He pointed to an archaic skyscraper on Wall Street. "My father's office was on the top floor there. When I visited him as a kid, I used to stand there and look down at the other buildings. But it's a strange feeling to be above it, looking down."

The pilot glanced quizzically at Whalen but said nothing as he guided the helicopter around the building and, flying over Battery Park, went all the way to the Statue of Liberty. There, trailing the wake of an oil tanker, he turned again toward Manhattan. "Okay, son," he announced, "we're going back home now."

At the heliport a police car stood next to the landing pad, and as Whalen stepped out of the machine a policeman moved toward him. The Heliways clerk stood nearby.

"Put your hands up!" ordered the policeman. Whalen obeyed. The policeman frisked him, found Whalen's wallet, and counted the money in it. "Look at this," he muttered. "This guy's carrying over two grand." He turned back to Whalen. "Where'd the money come from?"

"A bank," Whalen answered. "One we just flew over."

The policeman stared at him. "What are you talking about?"

"I got this money from my bank," answered Whalen.

"For what?"

"For killing—"

The policeman stiffened. "Killing what?"

"Time," said Whalen.

The policeman was not amused. "Where do you live?" he asked.

"Nowhere yet. I've just arrived."

"Where from?"

"Abroad."

"Got any identification?"

"Only money. Isn't that enough? There's no law that says I have to carry identification."

"Tell me more about the law and you'll sleep in jail tonight. Where is your family?"

"Dead."

The policeman nodded in disbelief. "You get one more chance," he threatened. "Where'd you get this money?"

Whalen shrugged. "From my bank, the National Midland, Wall Street branch." He waited. "If you don't believe me, call the bank's president, Mr. George Burleigh. Tell him I'm back in town, and he will tell you where my money came from. My name is Jonathan James Whalen."

The officer went to the office to make the call. When he returned, he handed Whalen the wallet. "I'm sorry about this, Mr. Whalen." He laughed uneasily. "You know, there are a lot of . . ." He stammered. "A lot of suspicious characters around." He paused. "Can I give you a lift somewhere?"

"I have no place to go to right now," said Whalen, and he turned and walked into the heliport office, where the pilot was lounging in a metal chair and drinking a cup of coffee. "How many helicopters, would you guess, flew over New York at the same time we did?" Whalen asked him.

"Five or so," answered the pilot.

"And how many people did they carry?"

"Maybe fifteen."

"Fifteen people looking down at twelve million," said Whalen. "That's quite a ratio."

The pilot leaned forward. "Pardon my asking, but what do you do for a living? There must be a secret—"

"There is," answered Whalen. "Money is the secret. The bank we flew over keeps it in trust for me until I reach a certain age."

"No kidding," said the pilot. "And when's that?"

"Tomorrow," answered Whalen.

4

It was evening. Whalen walked through the bustling streets of the East Side, and wherever he looked he saw young men and women, sitting or standing in sidewalk cafés and bars; leaning against their motorcycles, scooters, or cars; talking, laughing, embracing. They all seemed to be at ease with themselves and each other. Eventually he would have to make his way in their midst; he would meet some of them, judge and be judged by them, befriend them and be befriended in return.

He knew he must make a decision. Would he place himself among such people as their equal, and by doing so, remain slightly ashamed of everything about himself that would set him apart? Or would he enter their ranks as one whose position was of a different longitude and latitude from theirs—as a person who was his own event?

A girl walked toward him, her skirt swaying, revealing the shape of her long, tanned legs. Aroused, looking at her, he became aware of the space that his desire had opened between her and him, a space that a simple act of his will could not span. Had she noticed him, smiled at him, he would have found the courage to follow her, even to arrange a meeting. But she did not return his look. Still, he thought, perhaps he should follow her. But he didn't.

He walked into a restaurant. Mirrors reflecting the light from a crystal chandelier shot glittering prisms into even the darkest corners of the crowded room. Alone, he thought of Karen.

I've bought the smallest tape recorder available. It looks exactly like a match box, and it can record anything from a one-minute memo to a four-hour conversation. It operates on its own rechargeable battery, is activated by voice or hand, and contains an invisible condenser microphone that self-adjusts for voice distances even in a large conference room. I keep it in my pocket.

One day I might even want to leave it behind in Karen's apartment, and then claiming I left it by accident, pick it up the following day.

An American friend of mine once shared his apartment with his Argentinean girl friend for four months without letting her know that he was fluent in Spanish. By means of a miniature tape recorder that he concealed in his pocket when they were together or hid in the apartment when he went out, he would record her conversations, whether on the phone or face to face with her Spanish-speaking friends, many of whom did not speak English. In these conversations, his girl friend often talked about how much she loved him and what an unusually good and considerate man he was. But once in a while, on the phone with an intimate girl friend in Buenos Aires, she would candidly describe his lovemaking and bedside manners and speculate about his sexual preoccupations, fantasies, and fetishes, some of which she found peculiar and not to her taste. After listening to many tapes of conversations recorded in his absence, he became convinced that she was in love with him and felt reassured that there was no other man in her life. Nevertheless, unable to erase from his memory some of the poignant remarks she made about him, he began to feel embarrassment when making love to her and eventually became not only self-conscious but impotent. One night while caressing her, to end his misery he whispered to her in perfect Spanish how sorry he was that he had deceived her, and then he proceeded to tell her about the tape recorder. Shocked, the girl began to cry, and the next day told him that she felt betrayed. She said she could never forget that she had been spied on for months—and this by him, the only man she had ever loved and trusted. Soon after that, refusing to have anything more to do with him, she left for Buenos Aires.

"Look, man, I'm just trying to be friendly, that's all. Just now, I was standing behind you in line at the bank, right? And I saw you writing 'five thousand dollars'—not on a regular check or a bank form, but on a square little piece of paper—plain paper, nothing on it, right? Then you just signed this paper 'J. J. Whalen'—wasn't that your name? Whalen?—and you gave it to the cashier and he took that shitty scrap from you like it was pure gold. Then he comes back, all smiles, and just like that counts you out five grand all in that crispy cash! Now, man, I tell you, I been around banks, but I never saw a number like that: you sure got yourself some sonofabitch cash contact in that bank! Five grand for a shitty paper with 'J. J. Whalen' on it! Who are you, an underground numbers-game king?

"But listen, Whalen, let me clue you in on a truth about these sonofabitch bank tellers so they won't try to hit you with it one day. You know what the motherfuckers got going on the side, don't you? Some of them—like that fat black bitch who just gave you a come-on look—they take down the name and address of every old lady and widower, every faggy loner or rich bastard who comes in with a fat account. Then they sell the creep's name to certain guys who want to know where those kind of rich numbers live. Some of these guys pay up to a hundred bills for one good name and address!

"And believe me, Whalen, these guys are good at

making their information pay off nicely. One day, all dressed up as insurance men, they'll go see a sickly old lady, and they'll pull her by her ears until she gives them all that cash she keeps hidden at home, and all those gold crosses and old diamond rings. And there is no way for her or anyone else to know why these guys went after her.

"And d'you know about those dudes who have a nice thing going for them in the 'soul-saving' business? D'you know that if you want to split forever from that chick of yours who's got too sticky for your long hot finger, all you do is call a certain number, and they can save you a big hassle? You call that number and you tell the dude who answers that you've got a soul to be saved and he'll tell you where and when you should deliver the cunt. Then you tell your chick that you and her are goin' to look for a new place for the two of you. The minute you show up at that place and close the door, four motherfucking dudes will come in—and they're big, really big guys. They'll push you away like they're really mad, and they'll start playin' with your broad, kissin', nipple pickin', jerkin' off, and so on until you begin to fight them, just to show the chick you are all for her. The dudes will pick you up and take you out of there, but before you split they'll lay an honest-to-God hundred or so bucks on you for deliverin' that soul to them.

"After you split, the dudes will be pretty rough on your chick, particularly if she's tightassed about spreading wide for guys she wasn't properly introduced to, or if she doesn't dig sucking big mamas she didn't go to Sunday school with. Believe me, Whalen, she'll be roughed up like a soul in hell, front and back, top and bottom, until she learns how much true love is worth in this apple pie of a city. After that, a nice big dude will pick her up in his Caddy. If the cunt is nice, and if she walks the streets like her new daddy tells her and brings him all the stash that true love can make, he'll take good care of her. Got it?

"Listen, Whalen, what I'm telling you, man, is that—with your sonofabitch contact in this bank and mine with these dudes—you and I can score big.

"Now wait a minute. What's that gismo you keep on playing with in your pocket? Is that a cassette, man? Are you working for the cops, Whalen? I ain't saying anything more—and words ain't no proof, you creep. Man, I'm splittin' right now."

A recent nationwide poll claims that one-fourth of this country's adults believe that the position of the stars influences their lives. These people regularly read and consult daily astrology columns in newspapers, and they find purpose and meaning in the interpretation of their astrological sign. This is what the Astro Bio-Rhythm computer in the lobby of the American Museum of Natural History printed out for me after I fed a dollar into it, along with the exact moment of my birth.

Your fixed sign is Saturn. Saturn indicates feelings of separation and estrangement. You see humor where others don't. Having to leave familiar surroundings may well be a part of your destiny. Saturn also makes you hard on yourself. You are impulsive and have difficulty sticking to things. You must acquire patience and stability. You must protect your mental, physical, and financial resources. You have great gifts: do not squander them.

So much for the computer version of my fate.

And here is what I know: I can't decide whether self-awareness is a source of energy or of impotence. My real self is antisocial—a lunatic chained in a basement, grunting and pounding on the floor while the rest of my family, the respectable ones, sit upstairs ignoring the tumult. I don't know what to do about my lunatic—destroy him, keep him locked in the cellar, or set him free.

Since I left home I have been a vagrant, an outcast, living always in the present. Often I have regretted I was not brought up in the Catholic faith. I have yearned to confess, to have my broken inner autonomy cemented by means of union with that two-thousand-year-old institution of moral authority. But I have also realized that, however mystical, no church and no sacrament can protect me against the ultimate threat to my vital existence: losing the sense of my own being. Now, back at home, therefore, I must confront my past. Karen told me that she envied other people their pasts; she did not say she envied me mine.

If focused on closely, any moment of my life—even the one that has just ended—telescopes all that I need to know about myself, contains all my chances for the present and my prospects for the future. My past is the only firmament worth knowing, and I am its sole star. It is as haunting and mysterious as the sky overhead, and as impossible to discard.

On the crossroads outside Bangkok, during my playful moments I used to wait for the villagers to drive their carts home from the market.

The drivers, who smoked opium all day, trusted their

donkeys to find the way home, so by the time the carts reached the place where I waited, the men were asleep. As each cart approached, I would leap out of my car and patiently turn the donkey around without waking his driver; then I would watch the donkey trot away with the cart. One day I turned twenty carts around. Was I an instrument of each driver's fate, or were these drivers instruments of mine?

Some opium smokers rely only on raw opium; some mix it with dross; some, like me, have enjoyed both. Opium is unlike certain other drugs or narcotics in that one does not need to keep on increasing its strength or dosage in order to enjoy it. Whether with dross or without, opium gave me a sense of wisdom and balance, a spiritual tranquillity I had not known before I began to smoke and have not experienced since I've been disintoxicated.

Although smoking opium provides you with a sense that things are safe and predictable, the stuff itself seems crazy; it won't light up near the sea, it loses strength in the snow, it drips when the air is humid, and its potency changes from day to day. Opium does other weird things. In a man, it slows his sex drive but speeds up his heartbeat. In a woman, it slows her blood but speeds up her lovemaking. With time no longer your jailer, each pipe frees you: you inhabit a space where waterfalls turn into ice, ice turns into stone, stone turns into sound, sound turns into color, color becomes white, and white becomes water.

Maybe because opium is so unpredictable—only one pipe in ten producing the effect one desires—you never feel like an addict when you reach for the pipe, for the stuff might again refuse to please you. And when, like me, you don't smoke it anymore, you are not a past addict; you have merely abandoned opium.

I met Barbara, a Princeton dropout, in Rangoon. I introduced her to opium and she introduced me to several American and British expatriates, among them a Mrs. Llewellyn, who had remained in Rangoon alone after her husband, a British civil servant, had died there. One day Mrs. Llewellyn invited Barbara and me to lunch at her house, which stood sheltered by tall trees on a hill overlooking the Gulf of Martaban.

During lunch Barbara complained to Mrs. Llewellyn about the hotel we lived in, and when the old lady suggested that we stay in her house while she went to visit an ailing friend in another town for two or three days, we gladly accepted her invitation. Once a week a Burmese servant and his helper would come to clean the house, the garden, and the swimming pool. Otherwise, we would be alone.

I helped Mrs. Llewellyn ready her car for the trip, and she left the following day. From her terrace Barbara and I watched the ships in the harbor and the yachts criss-crossing the bay.

In bed that night, Barbara said, "It would be nice to own this house. We could live here, smoke our pipes, and not be bothered by anyone."

"I could easily get rid of Mrs. Llewellyn," I said.

"What do you mean?"

I shrugged. "Oh, I don't know. She's old and alone. No relatives, hardly any friends. And since she travels once in a while, no one would notice if she failed to come back."

Barbara laughed. "Don't be silly. This isn't a Hollywood horror movie. Go to sleep."

Later I tried to make love to her, but even though she had smoked a pipe shortly before we had gone to bed, she didn't respond.

The day Mrs. Llewellyn was expected back we waited up past midnight, but when she hadn't arrived by one we went to bed. An hour later we were awakened by the sound of a car. I told Barbara to go back to sleep; that I would help the old lady with her luggage.

When I awoke in the morning, Barbara was already up and dressed. "Where is Mrs. Llewellyn?" she asked.

"I don't know. She's not back yet."

"But we heard her come home last night, and you said you were going to help her. Now she's not in her room, and her car isn't here."

"I told you she hasn't come back," I insisted. "We heard someone else's car, that's all."

She became angry. "Stop playing games. Where is Mrs. Llewellyn?"

"I suppose she's somewhere. Everybody is. If I were you," I said deliberately, "I wouldn't bother about her anymore. No one will notice if she doesn't come back. The place is ours now."

Barbara stormed out of the house, slamming the front door. Through the bedroom window I watched her examining the unpaved driveway for car tracks and searching the adjoining garden. She came back, visibly upset, asking, "Where is she? What did you do to her, Jonathan?"

"Stop it. Let's go swimming," I said calmly.

Barbara put her hands on my shoulders. "What have you done to her?" she asked.

"Please, forget it," I said, pulling her toward me and kissing the inside of her ear.

She pushed me gently toward the bed.

"How did you—? Was it . . . was it quick?" she whispered. "What if they find the body?"

"Stop talking about her. This isn't a Hollywood horror movie."

"If I'd known you meant it, I never would have—"

13

"Let's go swimming," I said.

When we came out of the pool, naked, and I pointed to the cabana, Barbara followed me inside. Impatient, she threw some pool towels on the floor and lay down on them, her legs spread apart, her arms held up to me. I went down on my knees, my hands rubbing her thighs, searching her flesh. She was in a frenzy, trembling and shaking, her movements quickening as, urging me to take her, she arched off the floor, then fell back, then arched again.

"Don't—don't be gentle," she moaned. "Please be rough, Jonathan." For the first time in our lovemaking she was abandoned, no longer suppressing the desire that opium had heightened, probing my body, eager to feel me hardened. Thrashing under me, she yanked my hair, reached for my groin, tightened her grip on my flesh, bit my shoulder. Her orgasms came one after another, and she went limp and calmed down only after I reached mine.

No longer expecting to be interrupted by the return of Mrs. Llewellyn, we became comfortable hermits, for whom smoking opium was not a routine of slavery but a ritual corresponding to the rhythm of our life.

We smoked two pipes in the morning, one at midday, two in the afternoon, one in the early evening, and two or three at night, sleeping, eating, and playing with each other in between. We were attended to by two sons of my opium dealer, and these boys prepared our pipes, lit the lamps, and cooked our food. Our life had become smooth, effortless, and physically salutary.

Aroused by the opium, Barbara often provoked me. She would reach for my testicles and squeeze them until I smacked her. Then she would hit me back, and screaming abuses, she would stand up against the wall, smudging obscene words on her body in bright red lipstick. With no masking of what she wanted, she would encourage me to attack her. I would pull her down by her legs, and when she fumbled over me, we would struggle, each one trying to overcome the other. I left her alone only when, spent and exhausted, she could no longer move or moan. In the morning she would show me her bruises and insist that— to make up for the pain I had caused her—I tell her how I had killed and disposed of Mrs. Llewellyn.

In her opium haze, she kept recalling something I had once told her. I had visited a bordello on the outskirts of the city. There, as I sat among pubescent girls made up to look like young women and young women dressed to resemble pubescent girls, the madam noticed me glancing at an old woman, her face swollen and twisted, her disfigured body ravaged by opium addiction. "Do you fancy her, mister?" asked the madam, pointing at the woman. "I'm sorry for her," I said; "at one time she must have been as beautiful and fresh as these little girls." "She was," agreed the madam. "She lost her looks, but believe me, in bed she is still as hot as they are. Tell me, young man," she whispered, taking me aside, her perfumed breath warming my neck, "have you ever fucked a whore to death?" I laughed at her metaphor. "Don't laugh. You can do it here!" she said. "For two hundred additional American dollars, you can do anything you want with her." She pointed again at the old woman. "Anything at all." She paused. "Don't you say in English, 'till death do us part'? If you like her, you can part with her with your part," she said, pinching my loins. "At least she won't rot away, and she'll die like a human being—with enough money for a decent burial. I have a quiet cellar, ideal for such parting."

Now, thinking of the old woman, Barbara wanted to know whether I had taken Mrs. Llewellyn to that cellar. "Did you kill here there?" she asked. "Did you fuck her to death? Did you pay the madam to get rid of her body?"

Barbara began to suffer from insomnia and to smoke even more pipes than I. The pipe was her life, abolishing the difference between minutes and hours, between morning and evening. She lived surrounded by an invisible fence, and she wanted me inside it only to make love to her. Even in lovemaking she was eager to obliterate the confines of strict sex roles; she wanted to be both bait and baited. She liked to submit, to have her will expanded by surrendering to the will of her lover. Then she would change roles. Anchored behind me, she would tie my hands with one of her stockings, and holding me facedown she would excite me agonizingly slowly by letting her lips and tongue brush the base of my spine, halting just before my orgasm. Then, when I pleaded with her to continue, she would force me to lick her. When I slowed down or bit her, she would straddle my head. My face dampened by her groin, her nipples prickly upon my belly, she would run her hands down the length of my body, her fingers rough and unforgiving, yanking, rubbing, and jerking my flesh until, against my will, breathless in her own excitement, she brought me to an orgasm.

Opium and sex were our loves, but opium was the more possessive. It insisted on regimen, and on an even rhythm of activity and sleep, on hours set aside for the pleasure of food and the peace of the pipe. Our lovemaking steadily upset this required regimen and rhythm. We were betraying the opium, and the opium would punish us for our betrayal. It was time to quit smoking.

One morning, hearing a car pull into the driveway, we got up from the bed and dragged ourselves to the window. There was Mrs. Llewellyn, struggling to drag her large suitcase through the front door. Barbara tried to suppress her anger. "Why didn't you tell me?" she cried.

"Tell you what?" I asked. "That I gave the old lady money for a vacation in England?"

Back in the hotel, I was cold and sweaty. My heart fluttered and my pulse slowed. My body itched. I trembled. I oscillated between diarrhea and vomiting. Barbara's face was flushed, her pupils dilated; moistness blanketed her body. Her touch left my skin cold and damp. When we kissed, her tongue seemed swollen. Like me, she was ill. I was confused, not organized enough to summon help at first.

A few days later I called the hospital and asked for the ambulance to take us there.

After I was disintoxicated and released from the hospital, Barbara remained there, steadily receding under a sheet that was drawn tight across her shoulders, looking as though her head were separated from her body.

Her face was puffed and her body shrunken; her thin neck seemed unable to support her head. Her eyelids closed slowly, as if sticking to her eyeballs.

She murmured that she wanted to die, to take a needle and plunge it into her heart or, failing that, to jump off a tall building.

Even though I had provided and paid for the most competent doctors, Barbara died a month later from complications caused by her addiction. No members of her family in Nebraska could afford to come to her funeral, and at their request her body was to be cremated, her ashes sent home. A minister officiated at the brief ceremony, which was attended by one of Barbara's doctors, two nurses, Mrs. Llewellyn and her servants, and a minor official from the American consulate, who, knowing who I was, kept eyeing me with obvious interest.

The minister, an oldish, grayish American whose manner reminded me of my father's, spoke eloquently about those who, making their beds in hell, unable to rejoice or to seek salvation through their own spirituality, are in danger of being forever lost.

The essence of human life, he said, is as invisible as the meaning of a sermon or a book, or a notion of right and wrong, of justice and injustice, of love and hate. This essence cannot be depicted; it can only be hinted at and expressed through actions and objects, things that can be seen or handled.

Our consciousness, the minister said, is our sole spiritual compass; time and space merely provide a framework for the unfolding of our personal life—its suffering, sacrifice, hope, joy, and despair, which are our only reality. Only by accepting our spirituality as invisible, and the world as its expression, are we able to acknowledge the overwhelming presence of God, Himself an invisible power behind the visible universe—a power for whom space and time are, as they are for each one of us, forms of spiritual expression.

As I was listening to the minister, a single thought took possession of me: I've allowed myself to betray and mock life, to play hide-and-seek with the very essence of myself. For reasons obscure to me, I have failed to extract from my Protestant heritage its only prophetic and creative truths: that for as long as I live and in every situation, I must protest against the sin of distortion and the limitations of human existence, including the distortion and limitations of my own life and nature; that such protest contains both the hope of my spiritual rebirth and moral resurrection and the peril of uncertainty and personal confusion. Until now I've betrayed my sacred calling.

And I realized that in order to respond to this calling, I would have to begin with myself, with my own life. I would have to return home.

Whenever I am with Karen in a public place, among strangers, I feel an urge to touch her, to confirm my hold over her. At the same time, detached from the reality of the moment, I envision Karen and myself making love in the most outlandish manner, defying the taboos of society as well as the rituals we both still follow. Only Karen triggers in me a state in which I watch my own being as if from a distance.

Photography has never interested me, and that's why, instead of collecting pictures of myself, I collect and write down my memories and impressions. I expect Karen to do the same: after all, how much can I learn about her from her fashion photographs?

I still keep a letter Karen once wrote me.

To live in secrecy, Jonathan, is to fear yourself, to deny your own existence. You have made such a maze of your life that finally you no longer know what is satisfying: you live in an exile of your own making, excluding almost everyone, venturing out only in the name of exploration and expansion. Your psyche is your own POW camp and Barbara, the opium cipher, your prisoner. A woman who loves a man enough to give up a life of her own—but, denied his love, is given only sex—is dying inside.

That you have separated your love from your sexuality is what makes both your mind so keen and your life so tragic. You have risked many things, but not, it seems, your heart, and risking one's heart is the greatest risk of all. I have risked little, but with you I did gamble with my heart, and it was broken. With you gone I feel as if you were never here. You told me once that I was invulnerable, yet you set about to prove that I wasn't. When, finally, I succumbed to you, you blamed me for not being invulnerable—for caring about you and wanting you to care about me. And so you began to play that God-giveth-and-God-taketh-away Whalen game: get on your clothes, I don't want you anymore, you're getting out; sorry, I do need you, you're staying on; no, you're not staying, you're leaving now. You once said that with someone dumber than I, you would have been, as you termed it, "emotionally dishonest." For me, you said, you reserved your "spiritual truth"—which, to me, is nothing but a constant and cruel change of your mind. But in my short life I have discovered that truth is infinite and involves use of the heart. To illustrate: I love you, Jonathan. Has it ever occurred to you that your own heart has been ignored, denied, and subverted? Maybe your heart doesn't want to play any more Whalen games; maybe it just wants to be loved.

You know what pleases me: my modeling, being the best and the highest paid, travel, chocolate chip cookies, fucking someone I love—you—and hearing you talk about what it is that you would really want to do with me if I agreed to become your slave. But then I was weaned on peanut butter and jelly—salty goo and sweet mush: I'm an infant seer. I was never meant to be a slave, to be just fucked. I can't handle it. I don't know what it means. Mr. Prolong, the Don Juan of American virility and stay-hard bedroom power, whose only desire is to hear a woman scream either "More!" or "Enough!" makes me mute and frightened. My voice comes from mother's milk, from affection and warmth and support.

Karen measures love by its endurance and intensity. The spiritual loyalty of true lovers to each other has, in her eyes, nothing to do with their sexual faithfulness to each other, which she denounces as a dishonest state enforced by jealousy, a bondage of spirit, a reluctant acceptance of sexual inertia.

I recall that spring day when Karen and I lay on the grass in New Haven, kissing, reading, pulling up blades of grass. The wind scattered the long-winged nuts from the maples onto our faces, rippled through our clothes, blew Karen's hair across my face. Then suddenly Karen told me we were finished. She said she didn't want to see me anymore.

"New York is important to me," she said as she sat beside me. "It's my chance to have fun and to grow up. I have plans, Jonathan. I want to become a fashion model, one of the best ever, and to be free to dash off to Paris in April or Morocco at Christmas, to ski in Italy and Switzerland, to look at the black Goyas in Madrid. I'd like to meet men from England, Germany, and France. I want to sip warm beer in Dublin pubs and invite friends to dinner at my hotel suite in Rome.

"You and I keep thinking we need our independence. You're trying to free me, and I'm trying to free you. It has dawned on me that I don't want to waste any more time being miserable over you and our adolescent love affair. Don't blame it all on me, Jonathan. I'm as rational about it as you are."

Prior to her announcement, we had driven around in her car for hours. We'd run out of gas on a hill, and I'd stumbled down into the valley and climbed back up in a chill wind, a can of gasoline in one hand and a peppermint-stick ice-cream cone in the other.

After she said it, it occurred to me that one day my wealth could make it possible for her to become as free as she desired—free to create her own identity, free to impose order on all the circumstances and events of her life. Yet in accepting it from me, she would no longer be free to treat my presence in her life as the result of her free choice; rather, she would have to accept her new life as the calculated result of a choice that was initially not hers but mine. The cruel paradox of such a gift was that the very accepting of it would automatically diminish her freedom— her freedom in relation to me.

A while later, as I strolled barefoot around the lake, I saw Karen standing, her hair tumbled about, her pink and white striped blouse half unbuttoned. She walked to her car, the car door slammed, and she drove away. I kept on looking at the lake and wishing I could dissolve in it.

As a boy, I collected the cork tips of my father's cigarettes, believing they contained his unspoken thoughts and feelings. Now I collect my memories, hoping to discover the links between them.

The summer was ending. In Central Park the leaves had not yet turned yellow, but the air gave off a scent of decay. Layers of gray clouds hung low over the city.

Whalen drove along the Hudson River, past the docks with the transatlantic ships. He parked his car on a downtown pier and got out, scanning the riverbank until he found the spot he was looking for. He walked to the embankment, stood at the water's edge, and looked at the apartment buildings over in New Jersey.

Years ago, during one winter vacation, his parents had come to New York to see the new Broadway plays and attend all the benefit parties. Jonathan came with them, and to keep him company, his parents invited Peter, one of his grade school friends. One evening after his parents left the house, he and Peter decided to test *Never Say Die*, a book they had read about surviving under any circumstances, from being lost in the Sahara to fighting Russians on the steppes. For the test, Jonathan chose a night crossing of the Hudson River. Dressed in layers of sweaters and underwear, the boys took a taxi to an abandoned pier, where, reconnoitering the day before, Jonathan had spotted a crude rowboat left at the dock, perhaps by one of the dock workers.

The river heaved with chunks of ice. Through folds of fog the boys could see an occasional light flickering on the New Jersey shore.

Jonathan untied the boat and steadied it as Peter jumped in and sat in the stern. Then Jonathan climbed aboard, and as the current seized the boat and carried them away from shore, Jonathan braced his legs, dipped the oars awkwardly into the water, and heaving his body back and forth, began to row frantically. In the darkness, jagged pieces of ice banged against the trembling boat as it took them rapidly downstream. When they saw the lights of the Statue of Liberty and heard the horn of the Staten Island ferry, Jonathan realized that they were on their way out to sea. *Never Say Die* contained no instructions on how to save the crew of a small boat about to be tossed into the Atlantic on a dark and foggy night.

As the strong current swept them along the Manhattan shore, Jonathan could not control the boat. Tired and frightened, he loosened his grip on the oars, and sensing his surrender, Peter screamed and upset the balance of the boat. The boat turned sideways and capsized, throwing the boys into the water amid blades of ice and sloshing waves. Hanging on to the overturned boat, they drifted rapidly, then slammed into a pile of rocks. When Jonathan heaved himself out of the water, Peter was right behind him, but his body was limp. Quickly Jonathan pulled him from the river, and they both collapsed on the wet stone.

They climbed over an embankment and, cold and shivering, ran to the West Side Highway and crossed it. About two hundred yards down a street on the other side, the neon sign of a gas station glowed through the mist.

Behind it, high above the other buildings, Jonathan saw other lighted signs—among them the logo of his father's company at the top of the building that housed its Wall Street headquarters. Twice before, he had visited his father there.

Dragging Peter along by the arm, Jonathan stumbled into the gas station and asked the attendant to call them a taxi. But the sleepy attendant looked up at Jonathan only long enough to blink. In a loud voice Jonathan told him that he was the son of Horace Sumner Whalen, and pointed out the sign on the building. At that the attendant promptly got up and summoned a taxi, and the two boys arrived home long before Jonathan's parents returned from their evening out. In the following days, although both boys came down with fevers, neither Jonathan nor Peter mentioned their escapade to anyone. The attempt to cross the Hudson was Jonathan's first heroic attempt. It failed. Dodging the draft was his second.

Whalen got back in his car and headed north. At dawn he was driving past meadows and ponds in Connecticut. Turning off the main highway, he continued along a marsh road. The sun dispersed the mist that hung over the fields, and the car's wheels churned slowly in the sand. Scrub pine grew beside the road, and the green needles filtered the sun and dappled the hood of the car. He felt invisible and secure behind the wheel.

"Your mother was anxious to keep you abroad, Jonathan. In fact, she was desperate." The doctor avoided facing him. "In her nightmares you had often appeared buried as the unknown soldier. That's why she was pleased by your decision to leave the country before a draft notice could be delivered to you. As long as she and the company trustees didn't know your whereabouts, the draft notice couldn't be forwarded to you, and technically you were not legally liable. But your mother was very disturbed about not knowing where you were at any given time."

"To remain not liable, I had to be on the move, with no forwarding address."

"Well, yes, that's what was so upsetting. She imagined you with long hair and a beard, wearing army fatigues, high on drugs and hitchhiking through Burma, India, or Africa with only a knapsack and guitar." The doctor scratched his neck. "We tried to keep track of you—the best detectives from Burns took months to locate you, although at times we knew approximately where you were because you kept drawing money from affiliated banks by signing plain pieces of paper." The doctor grinned and looked at Jonathan. "As I recall, you wrote the last such check in Ankara—or was it Tripoli?—for something like thirty thousand dollars. In any case it exceeded your trust allowance for that period. Still, because you'd lived on less than half that for the previous two or three months, the trustees allowed the check to clear. Then your safari jeep was found abandoned. Your mother was frantic. Fearing you might have been kidnapped, and acting on my advice, she once again hired Burns detectives to locate you."

"How did they find me?"

"They traced you to a group of American hippies in Nepal. Apparently you had desecrated a temple; either you entered it naked, or you undressed inside—and there was a girl with you. A bank there that dealt with the National Midland managed to get you released from the local prison. Then we found out that you had settled in Rangoon and that, soon after, you became sick; you were either still smoking opium or already withdrawing, or maybe doing both."

The doctor put out his cigarette. "During that year your mother was hospitalized several times. To avoid unnecessary publicity, her nurse would call us whenever there was danger of an attack, and I would personally bring her here to the hospital. As your mother often refused to cooperate, even though it was obvious that for her own sake she should be under treatment, sometimes we had to"— he paused, searching for the words—"tranquilize her. Actually, though, she loved it here. She said she never wanted to leave. That's how my staff and I know so much about you, Jonathan.

The National Midland and the trustees called me continually. And your mother always spoke so fondly about you. She kept your photograph on her night table."

"What photograph?"

"You as a child standing next to your father in Whalenburg."

"How did my mother die?"

The doctor squinted thoughtfully. "It was an accident, really," he said.

"Did she kill herself?"

"Since your father's death, your mother had often been depressed," the doctor continued. "She kept all the medication I prescribed for her in small, clearly labeled bottles stored in her own special refrigerator in her bedroom. One day when the maid defrosted the refrigerator, the bottles got wet, and some of the labels slid off. That day, confusing the dosages, your mother simply took too much medication. Her death was a tragic accident."

"Was there an autopsy?"

"The law does not require an autopsy when the patient dies while under the care of a reputable physician. At the time of her death your mother was under my professional care."

"Why would my mother need your care *and* so many strong drugs?"

"When your father died, the demands that she considered her reason for living ceased abruptly. She became depressed because no one needed her."

"I did," said Whalen.

"Well, yes. But having failed school, the draft was upon you, and then you were gone. To your mother, this meant that even you had abandoned her. And so she died—alone."

I remember a luncheon given by the parents of one of Karen's college roommates. After lunch the parents went to their country club to play cards and golf, the other students went swimming, and I was left alone with Karen, who stood at the door watching the cars drive away. I pushed her hair back from her face and kissed her neck. She stood still and said nothing. I stopped, and we looked at each other. Her eyes moved lazily over my hair, forehead, eyes, and mouth. I slid my hands under her blouse, felt her skin, cupped her breasts. She pressed against me, her lips trembling, then quickly disengaged herself and, prompted by a quick decision, took my hand and led me to one of the guest bedrooms. Slowly, as if testing my control, she locked the door, pulled the window shades down, disconnected the phone from the wall, and took off the bedspread, folding it neatly.

I reached for her again and was about to kiss her on the mouth when she freed herself. Deliberately languid, Karen started to undress, slipping out of her dress, stepping out of her panties, kicking away her shoes. In seconds she was naked, lying on her back, her breasts heaving, her legs slightly bent. Uneasily I undressed, aware of her watching me as I stepped out of my trousers and briefs.

I lay on her, her taut body against mine. We kissed, and as she bit my lips and licked my tongue, I could sense her excitement, her wanting me. Just as I raised myself to slide into her, she told me to stop. She was not taking the pill, she said, because the side effects made her sick, and she had no diaphragm with her. I kissed her breasts, her nipples, guiding my hand over her stomach, the curve of her hip, rubbing my flesh against the inside of her thighs. I told her how much I wanted to have her feel me inside her, and that I would withdraw before my orgasm, but she resisted, whispering that waiting for me to pull out of her would kill her pleasure. As I moved down on her, she thrust her hips upward, inviting my tongue. My fingers inside her, I kept kissing and sucking her, but twisting and quivering, slowly she pushed me away. When I tried to hold her she pulled back, and covering her face with a pillow, she began to weep. After she had quieted down, I put my arms around her and asked why she hadn't come.

She said nothing at first, but after a moment she admitted that she couldn't reach an orgasm under pressure. With me, she said, she was too calculating, too anxious to please me and show how much she wanted me.

She told me about an African student, a gentle, softspoken black boy who had eyed her shyly for months but had hardly ever talked to her. He had finally offered to get some stuff for them to trip on, and one evening the two of them had gone to his room. They snorted coke and swallowed a sugarlike substance, and within minutes they started to trip. While Karen lay down, her world fragmenting, her will in tatters, the black boy seemed to solidify, and he became noisier and more excited. Dressed, then naked, he was all over her, his eyeballs rolling as he freed her breasts, then her hips, touching and kissing her gently, whispering how beautiful she was. All the while, she said, she was dreaming of being raped in front of him by me, whom he would then have to fight.

The man's sweat was oily; he smelled sour; and only when she noticed that he was not circumcised did she realize that he was naked and moving down over her face. He tried to enter in her mouth, but like a stubborn chipmunk hoarding a chestnut she kept her lips tightly closed, watching his eyeballs roll under his delicate long lashes as he rubbed his flesh, heavy and rigid like a stone, against her face, her neck, her breasts, coating her with his fluid. His fist between her thighs, he now tried to force her thighs apart, but she crossed her legs, stiffening like a taut canvas. Excited by his fist boring into her, she dreamt of letting go, of having an orgasm while faking that she couldn't have it. By now he was too high to know the difference; he was falling off her body, crawling onto her again. In his final effort he picked her up by her shoulders and turned her over, pinning her to the bed, trying to push her legs apart until her thighs began to burn beneath his thrusts. The two of them fell to the floor, but he found her again, entering her like a wedge. When she heard him moan and shake on top of her, she felt safe and loosened her limbs. Her orgasm shook her entire frame, the canvas of her body torn apart. She did not remember what happened next—or when her lover got limp inside of her, but it was with him that, for the first time, she became aware of experiencing two different kinds of orgasms. One came from being penetrated deeply again and again, the man's entire length and weight assaulting her almost painfully, yet in its steadiness and rhythm the assault becoming subservient to the rising wave of excitement that in one powerful moment would overcome her being. The other was brought about by her lover's hand and tongue on her clitoris, leading time after time to a frantic release that left her restless, as if yet to be fulfilled.

In the morning, terrified about getting pregnant, she went to the emergency room of the public health service where, after she told the doctor she had been forced to have sex with an older man, she was given a "morning after" pill and a checkup.

As I listened to her, I was overcome by a sense of futility: because I was, and always will be, part of her past, I could never absorb or influence her as a new lover. Suddenly I felt an overwhelming urge to break away from her past.

I stretched out on my back and forced her head down between my thighs. "Do it," I ordered her. "I don't care whether you want to or not."

I felt her hands running over my body. Getting up on

her knees and bending over my belly, she dug her fingers into my thighs. Her lips, then the tip of her tongue, drifted over me; she hesitated as she touched my flesh, brushing it against her cheeks, wrapping her hair around it, then, firmly, drawing it into her mouth. Her lips tightened around me, moving up and down, and she continued, her cheeks hollow from pulling, her hands stroking, her eyes wide open, watching me, gauging my response. I told her she was too gentle, and as if to smother her I pressed her head down, but she did not recoil. She was caught in her own rhythm, her body arching, racked with excitement. She kept swaying back and forth, her fingers clawing at my skin, but when she felt that I was about to ejaculate, she lost her balance and pulled back, hiding her face in the pillow. She did not cry.

Now that I have given Karen all the notes I scribbled during my travels abroad, I always wonder whether an incident from my past could one day alter what she has come to think of me. Since I have no idea exactly what that incident might be, perhaps I should have left out of my reminiscences anything that might sound nauseating or foul—or anything dull or banal.

I have steadily progressed from experiencing the sensations of being alive to expressing my thoughts about such sensations, as if pure expression were now the only original experience that I'm still capable of. But because language belongs to everyone, I suspect that whatever I capture in words becomes a fictional account—of me, as well as of someone else. There must be a place beyond words—a place of pure experience—to which I wish I could return.

After all the times I have been with Karen and made love to her, I still want her so much that I panic before each date at the thought that she might not show up. When she is with me and is about to undress or join me in bed, I can hardly control my craving to touch, to lick, to taste, to know, to enter her. Then my mouth is dry, my stomach is in knots, and my mind is seized by one thought only: to have her and to have her soon, sooner and longer, if I could, than time, the immovable guardian, will allow. I panic again when she is about to leave me. Then, when she is gone, I feel empty, without purpose, devoid of energy, anxious to see her again and, until then, to kill time lest my anxiety kill me.

At a cocktail party Karen gave the other day, I began to sweat from tension. A contest was taking place within me: one moment I was a controlled adult, the next a screaming child. A woman was telling me about her yacht; a man spoke of some investments; a couple told me they had known my mother. But I heard only Karen's voice: "I am going to forget you. Ours will be the only love I won't remember." I accepted a canapé and sipped my Scotch.

As a child I used to lie on the floor with my eyes closed and hope that, because I refused to see, I would become invisible and that people would walk past without noticing me. But I remember how upset I was when Anthony, my father's valet, did walk by without looking at me or even stopping to acknowledge my presence. What if Anthony did not like me anymore, I thought. I wanted to be at the same time invisible to those I feared and seen by those who loved me.

Another time I hid behind my father's filing cabinet and gave a scream. "Jonathan screamed," said my father. My mother replied, "No one screamed. We're late, let's go." I opened my mouth to scream again, to be found by them, but I couldn't utter a sound: what if my mother didn't want to hear me, no matter how loud my scream was?

Yet, I have never been able to lose myself. If one self failed, another was always ready to take its place.

Now I'm more than just visible; because of who I am, hundreds of people work to make my existence secure. My parents were the only ones who acted as though I didn't exist.

"I am fearfully and wonderfully made!" exclaimed one of my father's favorite Psalms. "What is man, that Thou art mindful of him?" asked another. But the *Britannica*, my father's favorite encyclopedia, answered by defining man as no more than "a seeker after the greatest degree of comfort for the least necessary expenditure of energy." If comfort is all that should matter to me, how am I different from an amoeba? And what has happened to the spirit, the only mystery and miracle of man's existence?

While I was in the hospital recovering from addiction, one of the doctors introduced me to the works of Abraham Joshua Heschel, the American Jewish theologian. This is what Heschel had to say about man.

In the eyes of the world . . . I am an average man. But to my heart I am not an average man. To my heart I am of great moment. The challenge I face is how to actualize, how to concretize, the quiet eminence of my being.

Beyond all agony and anxiety lies the most important ingredient of self-reflection: the preciousness of my own existence . . . and I resist the thought of gambling away its meaning.

The United States constitutes only six percent of the world's population, yet we consume over a third of all the world's natural resources. At home, half of the nation's income goes to one-fifth of the population.

My own situation is thus an extension of a larger economic and social disproportion. The company's researcher, who collected for me some newspaper clippings about the American superrich, came up with some interesting facts: over half a million Americans own assets worth a million or more dollars, and—I was amused to note—almost sixty thousand of them reside in New York.

There are only a few other Americans who appear to be as wealthy as I am. Until recently there were three about my age. The business of one, selling pet food and accessories, was started by his German-born father, who, after arriving in New York, opened a pet shop—one room filled with canaries—on Canal Street. So much for his family's contribution to America's greatness. The next in line, a shaving cream princeling, was a disturbed man. Periodically he would offer his fortune to the poor, but when thousands of them showed up at his door begging for help, he would withdraw and get high on hashish. Last year he blew his head off with a hunting rifle.

The youngest of the three is heir apparent to an old banking fortune. A health and nature nut, he occupies four floors of Chicago's tallest residential building, which he has turned into a solarium filled with livestock, soil, fertilizer, mulch, feed, pots, plants, and the latest in gardening equipment. At various times he has made passes at Karen, and once when she went to a cocktail party in his house he offered to give her a guided tour of his hothouse bedroom. She refused to follow him there. "Sniffing shit was not my idea of comfort," she said later.

And so here we are, the richest of the rich, all subspecies of American Mammon, each one, no doubt, wondering from time to time how to become great—since we are already rich. But how do I, the son of Horace Sumner Whalen, achieve greatness without attaining first what Thackeray called "the principal gift of great men": success? What kind of success can I still attain? Am I not, by virtue of who I am and what I own, a success already?

The recent *Dictionary of Occupational Titles* lists over twenty thousand specialized professions in America; being a millionaire is not one of them.

Our culture offers exciting, often desirable, archetypes: Politician, Explorer, Artist, Saint, Madman, Prophet, Murderer, Lover, Warrior, Sportsman, Messiah, Genius. But where, except on the *Titanic*, do we find the archetype of Millionaire?

As Oscar Wilde remarked, "Millionaire models are rare enough; but . . . model millionaires are rarer still!"

Would our collective memory and imagination preserve the sinking of the *Titanic* as vividly if, in the place of its colorful millionaires, the ship had carried nondescript, poverty-stricken immigrants?

But then the archetype of the millionaire is already implicit in our tradition and popular culture, which insist that to be rich is to be better off—if indeed not better—than to be poor. Our synonyms for the word *rich* include: independent, capitalist, swanky, productive, fruit-bearing, estimable, sublime, aesthetic, savory, delectable, nectareous, and harmonious. While synonymous with the word *poor* are the following: embarrassed, reduced, drained, distressed, inferior, trivial, sorry, contemptible, defective, worthless, vulgar, base, vapid, insipid, inept, lame, stale, dismal, and pitiable.

> The stronger the power of my money, the stronger am I. . . . Therefore what I am and what I *can do* is by no means determined by my individuality. I *am* ugly, but I can buy the *most beautiful* woman. Which means to say that I am not *ugly*, for the effect of *ugliness*, its repelling power, is destroyed by money. . . . I am a wicked, dishonest, unscrupulous, and stupid individual, but money is respected, and so also is its owner. Money is the highest good, and consequently its owner is also good. Moreover, money spares me the trouble of being dishonest, and I am therefore presumed to be honest. I am *mindless*, but if money is the *true mind* of all things, how can its owner be mindless? . . . Through money I can have anything the human heart desires. Do I not therefore possess all human abilities? Does not money therefore transform all my incapacities into their opposite?

That's from Karl Marx.

Am I, perhaps, my own archetype, a man who at any time can transform himself into his opposite?

If to live as one's own archetype is to be an artistic creation whose medium is the present, I should accept being no more predictable or controllable than any other work of art.

Then why not turn myself into a Sportsman? At one stylish New York dinner party I talked to a man who was a retired Olympic skiing coach. I asked him whether I could become, in one season, accomplished enough to reach the semifinals in the next year's American downhill.

"I'm not that good at sports," I explained. "Given my disposition—I'm a bit sluggish and don't like one-on-one competition—I need a sport that would speed me up by generating its own momentum and energy. I did a lot of skin diving in Africa, but I'm a terrible surfer. At Yale I failed in tennis, fencing, and handball."

"One question, Mr. Whalen." The coach seemed excited. "Why skiing? Why not gliding, or car or boat racing?"

"Because everyone would know that I could afford to have the best—the latest and fastest glider, boat, or car."

"And why the downhill?"

"It's straight. Man against himself and nature."

"You really would want to compete against the country's best skiers?"

"Not against. But why not with them? What do you say?"

The man got up and paced the room. "I don't want to discourage you, Mr. Whalen," he said, "but for such a crash program you'd also need the help of an orthopedist and a physical therapist. You'd have to build up strength in your feet, legs, and abdomen. We'd start high-speed skiing during the summer in Porfirio, Chile; then in early fall we'd go to Europe, first to glaciers accessible only by plane or helicopter, then, in the winter, to Chamonix, St. Moritz, Crans-Montana, Cortina, Val d'Isère. With this kind of rapid training, you would have to wear specially constructed devices to help protect you in high-speed falls. A battery-powered gyroscope—a model no larger than a bicycle wheel, which you'd carry while skiing—would have to be ordered right away. It would help you learn the turns. Throughout your training we would employ two assistants and two video cameramen, all expert skiers themselves. During every run you'd be filmed from different angles, and we would analyze your progress on a portable video screen. At the end of the day we would examine the tapes on a larger screen, to see you in greater detail.

"Barring a chance accident, by spring you could hire some of the past national downhill finalists and try to keep up with them. Then we'd hire some of the best French, Austrian, and Swiss professional downhillers—past Olympic and World Cup stars—to race against—or with—you." He stopped, convinced by his own arguments. "Yes, Mr. Whalen, I think it can be done, and I'm at your disposal."

My fear of violence began when as a boy I lay in bed and listened to my father rage. I couldn't bear it, and I think everyone, including my mother, my governess, even Anthony, felt the same way. Those few times I dared to disagree with my father, he struck me even if others were around. One night in our summer house, I wakened to the howling of Mesabi, my little dog. I put on my bathrobe and went outside. In the garden I found Mesabi with its legs tied together, and towering above it was my father, kicking the animal again and again. Seeing me, he explained that the dog had to be punished for disobedience and that the pain would break its future will to resist its master. I watched in silence, torn by pity for the dog, anger at my father, and hatred for my own weakness. After that, my defense against my weakness was to retreat to a world where I was the victor. I began to collect toy soldiers, and later, army and commando single- and doubled-edged knives and bayonets, among them many Nazi and Soviet World War II relics. I subscribed to *Soldier of Fortune: The Journal of Professional Adventurers* and read biographies of the great political, military, and business leaders, as well as stories about famous rogues, outlaws, and traitors, admiring only those among them who were orphans or who grew up alone, abandoned, or fatherless.

As children, Karen and I discovered sex together. We made up nicknames for genitals: chink for hers, bobolink for mine. She wanted to know where my bobolink was when I cycled. Did it lie along the top of the bicycle saddle or fall down on one side? Did it flatten when I lay on my stomach? I wondered how deep her chink was and whether it filled with water when she swam. Could it be sealed by tape? Could she hide money in it? Karen can still remember how one afternoon, as we played in the woods with other children, I put a branch inside her chink. One of the girls told Karen's mother about the episode, and Karen was spanked. Karen's mother, taking the fifty-cent piece I had given Karen to store in her chink, said it was dirty money from a dirty boy for a dirty thing. Another time, Karen tried to snatch my bobolink while I tried to deepen her chink with my hand. At first she screamed; then, as my fingers rested inside her, she grew silent and simply stared at me. Touching each other, we discovered sensations of desire that gave us far more pleasure than any plaything had ever given us. The desire was insistent, and it grew more insistent with each new opportunity for kissing and petting. Exploring each other gave way to feelings that demanded expression, that needed a language of love and devotion we had not yet acquired or developed. And so, to give drama to what we felt, we pretended to be characters from an imaginary fable: Karen was the beautiful and always difficult-to-please Lady Forsythia, and I, Lord Willow of Brook, was her proud though shy lover and defender.

Changing her voice, Karen would telephone my house as Lady Forsythia. Finally Mam'selle d'Arcy, my governess, feeling it was her responsibility to know about my friends, asked me how I had met this Lady Forsythia. "I was introduced to her by her friend, Lord Willow of Brook," I replied. "They're lovers, you know."

Now, even more curious, Mam'selle d'Arcy probed further. "And where did you meet this Lord Willow of Brook?"

"Where else but in the house of Yugo Slav?" I said.

"And who is that Mr. Slav?"

"Yugo Slav? A nice chap from Yugoslavia. He's also in love with Lady Forsythia."

Mam'selle d'Arcy was distressed. "You're so young, and already you know the strangest people, Jonathan," she moaned.

Although Karen talked freely about herself and described the sex she liked, I could not do the same; often I merely said yes or no to the questions she asked, or, silent, I would simply begin to kiss her, my hands moving over her shoulders and breasts, slowly and hesitantly descending toward her belly and thighs, stroking or kneading, teasing her flesh. Or I would start by sitting at her feet, stroking her calves, kissing and licking the inside of her knees, my hands and mouth grazing her thighs, circling around her flesh until she would start to force herself upon me, insistent and demanding, dictating my pace and the direction of my touch.

Karen once said that it's one thing if a guy is making it with a girl and she really doesn't know how far she wants to go and then begins to be afraid and draws the line. But it's another when a girl sets out to get finger-fucked and gives nothing in return. "Suppose you didn't want to get laid by a particular guy," I asked. "Would you still want him to finger you?"

"Why not?" Karen answered. "If I can get an orgasm out of it, I don't need any real fucking." She told me she was embarrassed and frightened by me only once, on our first night near the beach, but as soon as she felt my fingers inside her she felt only pleasure. It was the night of her first orgasm.

I remember a night we spent in a motel. Karen, who had downed a glass of straight vodka, was particularly free and abandoned, demanding to be made love to, trailing me even into the bathroom. She insisted on saying aloud all that we did to each other, all that she wanted me to do, and all that she suspected I never would do. Her onslaught left me, at first, excited, then deflated, too quickly spent. Annoyed with my embarrassment and my reluctance to satisfy her with my hand and mouth, Karen suddenly pushed me away. "You're hiding something from me, your lordship," she said.

"What?" I asked.

"A fossil in a glass case: yourself." Smiling despicably, she went on. "Do you recall, sir, how you died? Was it in a battle, in a victory, or were you taken prisoner and tortured to death? Better yet, did you die of an inherited malaise?"

This was my first defeat at her hands, and I've never recovered from it. After that, everything seemed to lack spontaneity, as if it were premeditated by an emotionally dead child. Unable to respond, I felt she had infected me with her own deadness.

I began to wonder: why did I choose a woman who cannot give of herself, whose love triggers in me a sense of competition and then makes me want to retreat? I see a ludicrous picture: it is after midnight; Jonathan James Whalen, the gray-haired, prematurely aged scion of Wealth, Health, Power, & Freedom Unlimited, is lying alone in his bedroom in his palatial home. Earlier in the day he has bragged to his psychiatrist that he has never conceded to a woman, yet Karen, his wife and the only woman he has ever desired, has for years preferred to sleep in a separate bedroom.

At one of Karen's parties, I talked to an attractive middle-aged woman, a contributing editor of *Branching Out*, a women's magazine. After telling me that she was in charge of her magazine's weekly report on sexual relationships, she said, "I'm going to stay away from you; otherwise Karen will think you've fucked me." About an hour later, in the hall, she brushed against me, kissed my cheek, and said, "I think you ought to know that I want you just for sex; let's leave the high life to Karen—she's so good at it!" She didn't attract me at all, but the notion that I attracted her aroused me. As I kissed her on the mouth, Karen walked in, took one look at the two of us, and turned away.

The guests wouldn't leave, so we drank beer and told stories until two in the morning. Karen ignored me the entire time. When everyone else had finally left, she turned to me and said, "Go ahead, fuck the bitch."

In bed, I was confident that I could change her mood. I hugged her. Sitting up, she slapped my face. "Cut it out," she shouted, "or I'll kick the shit out of you! Let me sleep." I felt humiliated. Karen's slap reminded me of a whore who once hit me when I told her she wasn't good enough for the price she was asking. In her tough, fuck-the-world way, she gained sexual control over me as a compliant woman never could, and I desired her even more.

The next day on the phone Karen said she wondered whether she should keep on seeing me, since obviously I had something serious going with the woman editor. To make my life seem as eventful as hers, I lied and told her she was right. When she asked if I was in love with that woman, I said, "No, but I'm not detached. To be with her and inside her, to have her all over me—it's impossible for me to screw and remain detached." I went on and on.

Before I left America, there were other men around Karen; among them was David, an actor with a larger-than-life quality. Stick your dick out the window and screw them all, on the table, on the carpet, against a wall, hump and jump and kick and lick—that was David. Once, in front of me, Karen, who was high on pot, said to him loudly enough for me to hear, "I would like to fuck you, sweetheart, until, until . . ." Then half joking, she dragged him into the bathroom and slammed the door. After a few minutes the two of them came out laughing, and when she asked him, "Will I see you again?" he answered, "I don't know. That depends on how bad you want it." I stood there—watching.

As a boy I had once received a note from my father on the subject of feelings.

You've apparently told your governess, Jonathan, that your feelings were hurt when I refused to let you travel on the company plane to see me in Washington. You and I both know that "hurt feelings" is nothing but a dodge for imposing one's will on another person. Your feelings are no more easily hurt than the feelings of anyone else.

When Karen fucked David practically in front of me, that was evil, but according to some theologians evil is the raw material of spirituality. Was Karen's act a way of prompting my rage and humiliating me for my self-control, or was she counting me out by deadening me even more? Was she giving in to desire, or to despair?

From the back seat of my limo I spotted Karen walking along Madison Avenue. I asked the driver to slow down and I watched her for a while. Casting quick glances at her reflection in the shop windows, she walked without a trace of slouch, her stride even, shoulders square, chest up, weight forward, arms and hands at ease, at times brushing her hair off her forehead and neck. As long as I have known her, Karen has been checking and rechecking the state of her image, as if it had a will of its own and could one day leave her. Equally on the street, at home, in a disco, or at a photographer's studio, Karen is fascinated by her own surface. She is a perfect symbol of our visual age.

In a disco, at her every step, mirrors split, enlarge, and multiply her image. If she adores disco dancing, it is only because it allows her to exhibit herself and observe herself at the same time. No matter that the endless beat deadens conversation, for her partner is usually as involved with his image as she is with hers. For me, dancing is an expression of elementary courtship, a crude pretense of sexual restraint, a publicly approved opportunity for exhibitionism. I have always hated dancing, and now I simply refuse to engage in it, although I don't mind watching others—particularly Karen—throwing themselves all over the place for my amusement.

My governess allowed me to watch TV for no more than five hours a week, and I spent my adolescence almost entirely without seeing it. Most of my American contemporaries, however, by the time they graduate from high school, have watched about twenty thousand hours of television, an equivalent of nine years on the job. As a result they're poor talkers and are easily fatigued by conversation. In constant need of adolescent distraction and entertainment, they find silence, reading, and solitary reflection synonymous with boredom. The disco, that noisy grave of human interaction, becomes the clinic for their never-ending withdrawal from an incurable addiction to television. The disco is their ideal playground: it kills language, it shrinks time, and it chops up awareness.

Many of my friends in India were mystics who believed that only by physical, moral, and emotional experiments can one discover one's intimate nature—and the nature of intimacy.

From them I learned that as a man can ejaculate without having an orgasm, and have an orgasm without ejaculating, so is he also capable of reaching one orgasm after another. To obtain such freedom and control, I mastered a technique of tightening and relaxing my pelvic muscles; I learned to cut off the flow of semen at the point of orgasm, allowing the pleasurable release of the climax to take place freely yet sustaining the tension and rigidity needed to maintain my excitement.

Later, my friends volunteered another revelation. A man who knows what he is after, they said, should never rely on pleasing his woman by just playing with her clitoris and fucking her. He must be able to keep his woman lying on her back while he, placed between her thighs, slowly pokes his hand, palm upward, inside her, and with his fingers following the delicate curves of her vagina, probes for the secret love-spot hidden on the abdominal side of her canal, between the pubic bone and the lump of the cervix. Through forceful squeezing and tapping of that love-spot the man can cause his woman to secrete a milky love-juice, which, during an all-powerful orgasm, she will ejaculate— as a man ejaculates—through her urethra. To many Indian mystics that juice is the woman's own semen, not much different in its substance from the semen of a man.

On dozens of occasions Karen has willingly submitted to my bringing her to this type of orgasm; on many other occasions she has reached spontaneous climaxes without, as I once crudely told her, lifting a finger off herself. In response, she said that a man who comes but cannot go is hardly her idea of a perfect lover; that, in fact, she considers my ability to hold off my orgasms, or to go through a series of them, a hang-up as morbid as the control it requires.

Now that I no longer depend on opium to slow me down sexually, I regret that I left India before learning how to deaden or—should I wish it—even eradicate my sexual urge. For even though sex is a veritable well inside me that drains me as I draw from it, ever since boyhood I have allowed it, several times every day, to absorb most of my energy.

One night she slid her hand along the inside of my thigh, and when, uncertain of her need, I didn't react, she turned away and said, "Good night, ice cube, maybe we'll clink against each other during the night." It was as though she'd forgotten how many times she had turned me down, as though, despite her apparent abandon, she weren't the most self-controlled and self-absorbed being I have ever known.

Another time, at the peak of our lovemaking, just before her orgasm, when with every fiber of my being I hung on to her and whispered I loved her, she pushed me away. "You've distracted me again," she snarled. "I'd better do it myself." And she propped herself against the wall, her legs spread wide, her hands buried between her thighs, probing her flesh. With her face flushed, her eyes vacant, her lips parted, she looked as if she were posing for a photographer, isolated from him only by the floodlights. Her fingers speeded up their frenetic search, her hands probed deeper, a grimace appeared suddenly on her face; gasping and moaning, she brought herself to orgasm, curled up into herself.

You might be pleased to know, Jonathan, that this week two of our board members and your former trustees have been called to high posts in Washington. James Abbott has been chosen to be Assistant Secretary for European Affairs, and Charles Sothern has been nominated by the President to be Secretary of the Treasury. Other members of the board have also had changes in their lives. Walter William Howmet, once your father's closest associate and an architect of our corporate growth, who has been until now chairman of the board, has also assumed the responsibilities of chief executive officer. Stanley Kenneth Clavin, another close friend of your father's and a member of the board, has decided to retire from his post as company president. Mr. Clavin says that with younger leadership emerging in almost every major division of the company, the new management should be free to work as a team. His place will be taken by Peter Baudley Macauley.

Is the above letter from Walter Howmet's secretary intended to keep me at bay, or is it intended to involve me in the company's doings? Either way, here I am, true royalty, the crown prince of American dreams, with power to effect changes in the lives of hundreds of thousands of men and women.

And I've gained all my wealth and power without risking my life in a war or a rebellion, without bravery or cowardice, betrayal, suffering, or sacrifice. Thus, as a dramatic hero I have no roots in Shakespeare, Dostoyevsky, or Stendhal. Am I merely an example of the banality of power and wealth in America?

A toothless old black man, unmistakably an addict, was sitting across from me on the subway. As two young policemen got on, he winked and mumbled, "I feel so good here, son, so good. You protect me." He rocked back and forth, attracting the policemen's attention. One of them came over and told him to get off at the next stop. "I'm just going home," he protested, "just going home." When the doors opened at the next stop and the man didn't move, the policemen shoved him off the train. It was my stop, too, and I got off and followed them along the platform. The policemen jostled the man, and when he fell, insisting that he couldn't get up again, they grabbed him by the arms and dragged him along the platform. I thought of coming to his defense, of placing myself between him and his oppressors, but I did not. It wouldn't have helped: the policemen would have turned against both of us with renewed cruelty. The man's shoe fell off, and one of the cops picked it up with the end of his nightstick and threw it onto the tracks. Only then did the other cop notice that I was behind them. He demanded to know what I wanted. "What did he do?" I asked them. "He threatened me," said one of them, smiling coyly. Then they walked away, leaving the old man on his back, his face smeared with tears and blood.

I jumped down onto the subway tracks and retrieved the shoe from under the third rail. I returned it to him, but he wouldn't move. "They won't let me alone, they be waitin' for me," he cried. He was on his knees on the platform, rocking back and forth, staring at the blood on his hands.

It occurred to me that I should lodge a protest against the police, but in any court of law my own past of addiction and draft dodging would only make me seem unreliable as a witness. I thought of finding shelter for the addict and paying for his rehabilitation, but such a gesture would have been only a rich man's arbitrary caprice, a further proof of injustice. Joining a political party devoted to the abolition of our unjust social order also crossed my mind, but it would have to be a Marxist party, I reasoned, and what did I, a penthouse resident and the ultimate scion of corporate democracy, have in common with Marxism, which, in the words of Marx himself, held private wealth to be nothing but "a eunuch of industry," with "*lack of moderation and intemperance*" as its true standards and "*fantasy, caprice, and infatuation*" as its only ideals?

A photograph of Karen entitled *American Champagne* made the cover of *Life*. It was by far the best, the most alluring, the most seductive picture of Karen I have ever seen, embodying all the magnetism that made her a true handmaiden of communal lust. Soon after it appeared, a caterer from Celebrities Cuisine, who was also an amateur photographer, claimed that he had taken the photograph— not the man who was credited with taking it.

The photographer who took credit for the picture was Karen's intimate friend. I had met him several times. In his mid-forties, widowed, he was an abrasive, restless, mean neurotic with the face of an angry hawk. He and Karen had known each other for quite some time, and it was obvious that he had been involved with her. What annoyed me more than that was that he treated her as if she were his protégée, and that Karen responded by treating him as if he were hers. He had once been a writer, but his paranoiacally gruesome novels—sexual quid pro quos concerning industrial society—had failed to secure a niche for him in the intellectual marketplace, so years ago he had turned for a living to his old hobby—female portrait and figure photography. As the retrospective exhibition of his photographs proved, he was undoubtedly a talented artist. When he first took up photography, he made a point of photographing ordinary women, often streetwalkers who were beaten down by poverty and misery. Many of them he photographed over long periods, up to twenty years, at two- to three-month intervals, starting when they were in their early teens. Owing to his obsession with these common women, he often managed with his camera to extract from them that uncommon beauty that sets each being apart from all others. Next, heralded by newspapers and magazines as the Kafka of the portrait and the Gogol of the nude, he became a favorite among advertisers and art directors. After that his allegiance, and possibly his obsession, changed. Now he photographed only women of uncommon beauty, society's supermodels and actresses. But as beautiful as they all were—and Karen was one of them—his art failed to discover what was unique about each of them; in his photographs they all looked flawless—but a bit alike, and common.

The caterer agreed to see me, but only after I had told him that I was a close friend of Karen's. Born in Poland, he was a skinny, aging man who spoke with a staccato accent. His lifetime ambition was to become a professional photographer, but his wages did not allow him the extravagance of hiring professional models, and until he took the picture of Karen, all the women he had ever photographed— nude, exotic, large-breasted—were really men—transsexuals or transvestites who posed for him out of vanity. He had made an effort to exhibit, and initially his photographs had proved quite a success with viewers and critics alike. Just as three of his widely exhibited pictures, entitled *Woman I*, *Woman II*, and *Woman III*, were about to be reproduced by *Century*, the nation's most prestigious art collectors' magazine, someone—possibly one of the models— leaked the information that Women I, II, and III were, biologically, men. Fearing public ridicule, *Century* changed its plans and rejected the photographs, and the caterer's chances of becoming a professional photographer sank once again to zero. Then one night when he was overseeing a dinner catered by Celebrities Cuisine, he saw Karen, who was one of the guests, being followed and photographed by the man on assignment from *Life*. At one point the *Life* photographer left the party for a few moments to try to find a parking place for his car, which he had double-parked in the street. As he dashed away, he left his loaded camera in the custody of the caterer.

During the photographer's absence, Karen, egged on by a raucous crowd, attempted to open a magnum of domestic champagne. When the cork flew out, Karen was soaked by a jet of foaming champagne, and the caterer couldn't resist snapping a few pictures of her with the camera left in his care. When the *Life* photographer returned, the caterer handed him his camera without a word about the pictures he had taken.

Soon the fetching picture of Karen soaked in champagne appeared on the cover of *Life*, and certain critics called it the most successful cover in the magazine's long and distinguished history. The caterer then came forward and said that if Karen would testify on his behalf, the credit for the picture would launch him in a photographic career and fulfill his life's dream.

In most arts, the artist remains physically detached. The writer starts with words, the composer with sounds, both of which, by nature, are abstract, yet which can trigger in the reader or listener concrete images or emotions. But a photographer starts with the concrete; in the immediate confrontation between his camera and his subject, the abstract is yet to be born. Thus, one can easily understand the caterer's frustration and grief at being denied the truth of the existence of that confrontation.

Nevertheless, the *Life* photographer categorically insisted that he and he alone had taken all the pictures of Karen that evening. And because neither Karen nor any other guest seemed—or wanted—to recall seeing the caterer take the now famous picture, the matter was put to rest, and with it the caterer's prospects for a career in photography.

Karen's *Life* cover led to a thirty-second spot TV commercial, in which she opens a bottle of California champagne and, as we all watch, gets soaked by it. As a result of the success of that TV commercial, she was also offered a small role in *Totem Taboo*, a Hollywood movie.

Even though I had no doubt that it was the caterer who had taken the *Life* cover photograph of Karen, I knew that his chances of proving it were nil. "I have always wanted to own a photography studio," I said to him. "If I were to acquire one and finance its operation, would you be willing to accept a contract that would guarantee your employment and creative independence?"

He looked at me in disbelief. "But why—why would you do such a thing? That's a lot of money. It will take a lot of planning, and I might never be able to pay you back."

"So what?" I said. "My plans for the future have always turned out to be made for the past."

A month later I owned one of Manhattan's better-located studios, and the caterer ran it with the sureness of an old pro. The word that big money was behind him spread through the city, and soon customers were flocking to him. Thanks to the secrecy I insisted on, nobody, not even Karen, knew the studio was mine. The proof of the caterer's success came when Karen, recalling that I had once met him, asked me whether I could introduce him to her. The man was on his way to becoming the best portrait and figure photographer in the business, she said, and inasmuch as she was the best model, it was time the two of them got to know each other.

"I'm so glad to see a fine young man like you, Jonathan, coming to pray at your father's grave, God bless his soul. But you know, Jonathan, even cemeteries aren't what they used to be. I mean yesterday there was this broad putting the make on this guy right here in a graveyard. Since I started working around here, I've seen a lot of different folks with a lot of different feelings, usually crying or just plain sad, but that broad was just plain horny. And there she was, I don't know, about twenty, beautiful body, long hair, with this dude about twenty-five, maybe not even that. They weren't mourning, let me tell you. And then right there, next to your father's grave, God bless his soul, he's got one hand on her tit and the other on her ass. I couldn't believe it. Like it was really sexy seeing this chick worked up, you know? I kept wondering what those boobs felt like. I felt like jerking off myself right then and there, and I hope your father would forgive me for saying this. It's the truth."

The other day Karen remarked that while no profession could make me any richer, becoming a professional gambler could certainly render me poorer. I know that Karen likes gambling, and I know that some of her better-to-do friends occasionally stake her to her little games of chance in the casinos of Atlantic City and Las Vegas, in the Bahamas, in Europe.

For me, however, the gambler remains as unskilled as the assembly-line worker: he can no more influence the outcome of the cards or the wheel than the man on the assembly line can alter the design of the product. All either one can do is repeat a short activity which is meaningless in itself over and over again.

In the eighteenth century it was mainly aristocrats who gambled; given their adventurous and unpredictable lives, the very repetition involved in gambling probably provided them with some sense of reliable patterns. Today, however, gambling is primarily the domain of the working class, who feel comfortable because the game is as familiarly repetitious as their work, but who at the same time seek in it an easy escape from their own existence to a less predictable one.

These days I manage the details of my life in an orderly, almost predictable fashion. I eat regularly, either at my hotel or in the best restaurants; I exercise in the hotel gym and swim in the pool; and I've gotten rid of my acne. I note all my appointments on my calendar, along with lists of things to do and to buy, and neatly cross off chores as I complete them.

I now control my entire inheritance and meet with half a dozen lawyers regularly to settle the details of my affairs. At our first meeting I realized that these vassals of my payroll provided me with equal representation of the Protestant, Catholic, and Jewish faiths. At a time when nearly one-third of America's youngest children live in families earning less than the median income and never receive such basic medical care as immunization and other simple treatment for the prevention of disease, these lawyers from Yale, Harvard, and Princeton were still sufficiently indoctrinated by their Ivy League education to view me as the quintessential product of the work ethic rather than as merely the inheritor of millions—that is, an aberration of the working of this ethic. Nevertheless, familiar as they were with the details of my past, I could also see that they had difficulty hiding their curiosity about how ethically Protestant the child of Horace Sumner Whalen had turned out to be.

As we sat eyeing each other politely, I was reminded that the prime function of these lawyers, like that of company managers, is to represent this country's business elite.

Calvin Coolidge, a lawyer and a president, once quipped that "the business of America is business," and my father was known to say that his company was known by the men it kept. However, a recent nationwide survey of American business managers suggests that business—the heart of America—is ailing. Half of all the businessmen polled asserted that they found their work utterly unsatisfactory; one-third said that the strain of day-to-day business hurt their physical and mental health; and over seventy percent admitted that in order to conform to the standards established by their corporate superiors they frequently had to compromise their personal principles. No wonder, then, that in order to escape such growing business pressures, the average American watches television almost seven and a half hours a day.

So much for the work ethic of our success-oriented business elite. Equally revealing were the findings of other polls. Even though hypertension affects millions of Americans and heart disease is the nation's number-one killer, only one percent of the public is aware that the control of high blood pressure is a necessary step in combating heart disease.

I was tempted to ask my lawyers what they thought

about the state of this nation, but all I said was "Well now, gentlemen, let's talk about something that's a real high." I paused and glanced at their well-cut suits, and they all froze, fearing I was about to mention opium. "My income," I blurted, and they all chuckled, those six clean-shaven college kids put at ease by their unpredictable master.

Glancing through an illustrated magazine, I ran across a picture of Karen posing naked in a full-page advertisement for some hygienic preparation; her arms were crossed in front of her breasts, and her hands were folded between her thighs.

When I voiced annoyance to Karen about the ad's demeaning nature—"Antibacterial" was written next to her face, "Antipruritic" next to her neck, "Anti-inflammatory" next to her breasts, and "Antifungal" next to her belly— she angrily told me that her job was to model for the advertisers, not to question their taste. I countered by pointing out that although she often censored what she considered to be my antifeminist attitude, yet she found no fault with this ad, even though it used only a woman as the host of various body pollutants which, after all, affect both sexes equally. The incident made me aware of how proud and determined Karen is. She insists on working even though, if she would agree to share my income, she wouldn't have to. Ironically, her independence is one gift I cannot buy her.

Maybe because she insists so on her independence, I don't feel overly sympathetic when Karen claims to be exhausted from her work, or when she says she doesn't feel well. Several times when I've been at the bank settling my estate, surrounded by people who were obviously eaves-dropping, she's called to break our date for the evening. In such circumstances I haven't been able to express my indignation freely. On two occasions I had been looking forward to spending a couple of days with her, and both times she called it off only a few hours beforehand. This erratic behavior I know to be habit with her, but still it suggests that other people and events are more important to her than I am. Is our being together so exhausting that we can see each other only when we are both well rested? Must we assume that after each meeting we have to go back into our private lives to recuperate? Yesterday when she called to cancel another date, I was unresponsive once again. Karen's rejection sets off torments within me. Instinctively I retreat instead of exploding, however, lest I obliterate my chances for whatever may happen next.

"I was vacationing with my family in the Adirondacks, Mr. Whalen, when Dr. Frederick, your mother's physician, telephoned me. He asked if I could interrupt my holiday and join Mrs. Whalen in Spain right away. Apparently your mother had radioed him from the yacht during the night, and the doctor could tell by her tone that an attack was imminent. As your mother's nurse, I was qualified to be with her during such an emergency, so I promptly flew to Madrid. From there your family's company arranged for a private helicopter to ferry me to the yacht, which was anchored near the island of Formentera.

"Your mother was in a bad state: incoherent, flushed, possibly drugged. Apparently, just before I arrived, one of her guests, a middle-aged American art gallery owner, had invited one of the sailors—a teenager—to his cabin, where he had given him a powerful narcotic. While the boy was under the influence of the drug, the guest repeatedly assaulted him sexually. The boy was then moved to another cabin, where crew members found him hallucinating from the drug and bleeding badly. The whole crew had taken the boy's side, and they were threatening to radio for the police unless your mother, as well as the gallery owner, immediately paid substantial damages to the boy. Fearing an international scandal, the captain sided with the crew. Your mother, feeling threatened, became a bit paranoiac and difficult to handle. She was furious that I had come, and she wanted the helicopter to take me back. When I refused, she ordered the crew to detain me in a cabin. I showed the Spanish captain Dr. Frederick's instructions, as well as the medications I'd brought with me, but the captain refused to cooperate with me. Most of her guests, too, even though they realized how sick she was, took her side. Finally she became hysterical and locked herself in her cabin. From outside we could hear her throwing herself around the room, and only then was I allowed to intervene. I tried to talk her into coming out, but she wouldn't.

"Finally I persuaded the captain to force the cabin door open, and when we entered your mother attacked us with hairbrushes, gin and vodka bottles, vials of drugs, books, even her brooches and necklaces. Screaming obscenities at the captain and me, she threatened us with a marble letter opener, and she would not allow me to get close enough to give her an injection.

"Even though I was accustomed to dealing with Mrs. Whalen's violent outbursts, I began to think that I would need assistance. But eventually your mother weakened. Pale and bruised from falling, she began to tremble and vomit. Like a sick child, she asked for help, and when I went to her with the injection she no longer fought me.

Worried by her condition, the captain radioed your family's company for help, and the helicopter soon returned to pick us up. I packed some of your mother's belongings—among them a photograph of you standing next to your father—and we flew to Madrid, where a chartered jet was waiting to take us to Pittsburgh. A private ambulance took us from the airport to the hospital, and a day later I returned to the Adirondacks to continue my vacation. I was quite exhausted."

"It's no different from operating any other large gadget, Mr. Whalen, and for a young well-to-do man like yourself flying a glider could be a lot of fun—or, as they say today, good therapy. Gliders are just big fiberglass ballast tanks equipped with all kinds of easy-to-read instruments. It takes no time to learn which levers are for flaps, which for gear retraction, tow release, and landing parachute. Then there is an altimeter, a compass, oxygen gauge, and so forth. It's not as complicated as it looks.

"When you first get going behind the tow, you feel like a heavy bird that can't quite make it into the air. Then, when you are only a few feet off the ground, the wings bend up at the ends like a bow and lift the fuselage into the air. Finally, you pull the tow release and retract the landing gear. Now all you hear is the wind, and all you see are clouds puffed up around you like cotton balls.

"You swoop up and down, and clouds swirl as you rush toward them. The glider, as it gets up to a hundred and forty miles an hour, begins to tremble—but you do not; you nose up and everything's peaceful again. The best part of all is that perfect mixture of feeling safe yet knowing that just one little thing going wrong can shake you apart."

Having realized that to practice a sport is to turn ordinary experience into personal drama, I once became a sponsor in an international sand-yacht race in East Africa. I watched the dozen yachts take off as if catapulted from a single slingshot. Slender kayak-shaped plywood bodies with tall masts and bright sails, they moved on three wheels that were fitted with treadless tires, the front wheel linked to a tiller that fell neatly between the racer's knees. As the yachts sped along the strip of hard-packed Ukunda beach, the flutter of their sails stirred up birds and monkeys that were hidden in the dense bush. Reaching the far end of the beach one after another like pale dots of color dissolving in the heat, the yachts turned back, into the wind now, askew to the ground, one side wheel skidding over the shallows, the other high up in the air. Sails close-hauled, the yachts tacked diagonally, rushing at the wall of the jungle, making the monkeys shriek with fear and dive deep into the bush and the frightened birds fly off. Then the yachts turned again toward the ocean, side wheels going up over the shriveled roots of the bush, then touching the sand, and once more the monkeys returned to their watching posts.

Just before the finish, the racer I sponsored lost control. During a sharp jibe his yacht overturned and one wheel broke off, rolling into the bush and striking a snake that was wrapped around a tree trunk. The thin ribs of the smashed cockpit pierced the man's chest; his blood seeped into the sand and onto the yellow sail. The snake slithered across the beach, circled the wreck, then coiled itself around the broken mast.

After the race, a European racer on his way overland to Zanzibar agreed to let me join him. We took off in his old safari-rigged jeep for Dar es Salaam, but at dusk we left the roadway and drove along narrow jungle trails toward the ocean. In the rapidly descending darkness our headlights picked up the glowing eyes of jungle cats. While the sand was still warm, we stopped on the beach and spread out our blankets beside the car.

Before retiring, the racer turned on a bright carbide lamp, opened a small plastic bag, and removed a bottle of isopropyl alcohol, a thin glass vial, a tiny disposable syringe, and some cotton pads. I watched him disinfect his left forearm and fill the syringe with white fluid from the vial. Running the short needle carefully up under the skin's surface, he slowly injected the fluid into his arm. He explained that he was using a vaccine to counteract a rare virus that was damaging the optic nerves in both of his eyes. The virus could cause blindness, so a vaccine was required to counteract it, and since there was no commercially prepared remedy effective enough to kill the virus without severely damaging the eye itself, the doctors had recommended a vaccine made of his own virus.

The vaccine was prepared for him by a researcher in the laboratory of a well-known New York hospital. When I asked if there was a risk in taking such an untested vaccine, he answered casually that if for any reason his organism failed to develop defenses against the virus, the same virus might also attack other organs; suddenly stricken, left without prompt medical attention, he could die. Nevertheless, each week he increased the vaccine dosage, hoping his body would combat the virus and thus save his eyesight.

"How many of these injections have you already given yourself?" I asked.

He watched the growing redness on his arm. "Eleven. I'm increasing the dosage significantly again now."

"Don't you think," I said, horrified by the prospect of seeing him incapacitated there in the jungle hundreds of miles from any human settlement, "that you should be somewhere near a hospital, or at least near a doctor?"

"I do," he replied, looking at his watch. "Fifteen minutes," he said calmly, replacing the vial in the bag, "and I feel fine. I guess I won't get sick from it this week. And don't you worry about my vaccine; while we're asleep, you or I could be bitten by a venomous snake. Now, that can really be lethal: your jaws lock, your eyelids refuse to blink, your lungs stop taking in oxygen." With that he extinguished the lamp. I lay for some time listening to the jungle noises, thinking of the snake looped around the mast.

The next day, as we drove through the dense underbrush, he pointed to a couple of native children wandering alone far from their village compound. "Children are often kidnapped here," he said. "Child poachers come from all over in rented safari vehicles. They take solitary trails off the main roads where they can grab an unsuspecting girl or boy. Sometimes they violate the child on the spot, even kill it and leave the body in the bush to be devoured by jungle animals."

"How do you know all this?" I asked.

"I like children," he answered, laughing.

"You may recall, Mr. Whalen, that these debentures became part of your holdings when the trustees decided to sell your interest in Tinplate to S.F.I. Would you be willing to tender all or part of them for common stock? The income would be less, but the stock would represent a more attractive growth investment. The offer would be three point two shares of S.F.I. common for each hundred dollars of debentures. That would represent about seventy-five dollars' worth of common stock for debentures that sold recently at sixty-eight dollars and earlier this year for as little as fifty-three dollars. Of course, whether the other debenture holders will accept such an offer depends on their opinion of S.F.I.'s market strength. As you may know, its shares have moved extremely well lately, and that means there is a risk of profit taking by the common stock shareholders. If all the debentures were to be tendered, S.F.I.'s balance sheet would certainly look a good deal better, with its debt decreased and its equity increased. Additionally, the number of S.F.I. shares outstanding would increase almost three times, and much of the leverage, which made the stock so attractive to begin with, would be lost. It is a question of balancing the gains against the risks—"

"I have no idea what you're talking about," said Whalen. "When do you need my answer?"

"The advantage of your situation is that there is no pressure on you to decide. However, since you are the majority stockholder, your eventual position will have to be determined—"

"I understand," said Whalen. "Let me find out about it."

"Certainly. Certainly. Our financial and legal departments will gladly assist you at any time. Of course, you're free to seek advice from the outside. Just call my office and let me know."

"There's something I *would* like to know."

"Yes?"

"At present, who is the company's second-largest individual shareholder?"

"It is Walter Howmet, sir. He was a close friend of your father's and is now chairman of the board of the company. Would you like to meet the Howmets?"

"I already have. They're my godparents."

Whenever in my thoughts I reach back to the time of my disintoxication, I recall the surroundings and the people around me but not my state of mind. Was I in pain? Did I long for a pipe? Did I drift from hour to hour and day to day, oblivious to what I thought or felt? And since I don't recall my feelings or my pains, how am I to know what I have inherited from my ordeal? What if it has given me nothing but the memory of the events? If that is all I have, I would rather invent my past than recall it.

But what if I have cut myself off from feeling any pain at all now? Each time I stand near a window high up in a tall building, in a momentary reflex I want to smash the glass with my head. I imagine it in slow motion: my blood reflected in thousands of tiny shards of cracked and splintered glass that cascade to the ground. I hear the screams of people far below, the braking of cars, the commotion caused by the falling glass. What I can't imagine is my pain.

In a health journal I found the pharmaceutical manufacturer's advertisement for the medication the doctor recently prescribed for me after I complained about my easily irritated colon. The ad warns that the drug is strong enough to impair alertness, that it increases response to alcohol, and that it might lead to suicide. Because of this, until satisfactory remission has taken place, close supervision of the patient who takes this drug is essential.

For a moment I assumed that my doctor had made a mistake. The drug sounded so powerful that it should obviously be taken only by the most gravely ill. But then I read the following list of symptoms, which the manufacturer recommended be considered by a doctor prescribing the drug: the patient might display repeated lip biting, a tense facial expression, and moist palms; his fingernails might be bitten down; he might complain of waking early in the morning; he might be agitated, restless, and irritable, finding it almost impossible to start work in the morning; he might suffer from a nervous stomach, lack interest in most things, and feel tired and listless most of the time.

Is that all? Yes. But most ordinary people display some of these symptoms daily, even without undue stress. Moreover, the symptoms seem minor indeed when compared with the impaired alertness and the other serious side effects caused by the drug meant to remedy them. If my father— just because he was "agitated" or "complained of waking early in the morning"—had repeatedly been given such a drug, would the impaired alertness caused by it have allowed him to become one of the giants of industry?

Centuries ago, in certain countries, the king and the ruling elite would fill many important government posts, not with native-born subjects, but with suspicious aliens— religious converts, political traitors, dissident émigrés, men captured as boys during military raids abroad who had been raised as strangers among the natives; in short, renegades. This policy was based on the belief, often verified by history, that the renegade, having escaped or betrayed his past relationships and therefore unable to go back to them, was very likely to make a trustworthy and loyal subject, one who would have to struggle and connive to succeed and who would therefore be less likely to betray his new country and religion than a native would.

Exiled from opium, unwilling to go back and vegetate abroad, at times I tend to see myself as a resident renegade—my motivation heightened by my return to the States, which while it is my home is also the country of my lasting exile.

My self-doubt often makes me feel that I might never be able to carry off anything original and that my independence, my inheritance, my relationship with Karen all demand creativity I don't have. Before I came back to American I had resigned myself to respond to situations, not to instigate them. I had accepted myself as being alone. But now things have changed. It seems that what I really need is a drug that will increase my consciousness of others, not of myself.

Once when I was considering going through psychotherapy, Karen warned me that it is a bit like the treatment for a broken shinbone that has mended crookedly: to correct it, breaking the bone again is often necessary. But, unlike bone surgery, psychotherapy offers no anesthesia, no clearly defined period of healing, no assurance that things will ever mend, and for a while your new walk might seem like a limp to you and those who know you.

Karen suggested that joining a psychotherapy group, even for one weekend, would give me some sense of what other people—men and women from different walks of life—think of themselves, of me, and of the world around us.

Since I have always suspected everyone who likes me of having poor judgment, and often despised them for being so easily taken in, I decided to take Karen's advice.

A psychiatrist friend of Karen's recommended an encounter group that was planning a weekend in Lake Success. We met early Friday evening in someone's country house. There were fifteen of us, an uncomfortable assortment, seated around a long table on straight-backed chairs. At first I felt superior to the others, assuming that no one else could match my experiences abroad. How could these supermarket psychotherapists understand what I had gone through?

In the course of our discussions throughout the weekend, two or three people did admit that my image was intimidating. A man from upstate said he envied my independence and wealth. Another man said he would be frightened if he had all my money. One girl said she would not want to go out with me. A woman history teacher from New York University, who at first seemed gentle and shy, turned out to be the most belligerent person in the group. She accused me of leading a life based on distortion. How could I possibly depend on others, she demanded, when my position was forever forcing me to use them as servants?

A girl who had recently graduated from college broke down and cried. Her boyfriend was black and schizophrenic, and she was torn between her own reality and his. She said that she often had to listen to his secret whisperings and enter his odious world. She sometimes even slipped into his fantasies, and at such times if she saw anyone looking at her, she believed that she was a white Negress.

One of the black people in the group said he felt smothered because he was unable to express his emotions. He said his lack of education prevented him from even articulating his own problems. He kept mumbling, "I don't make sense, I don't make sense," and when we tried to convince him that he did, he countered, "How do you know? You haven't lived my life. If my story makes sense to you, then it's a lie, because it shouldn't. It's a black man's story, not yours!" I felt moved by his anguish and his sense of entrapment among us, but despite my compassion I remained detached from him and from the group, aware that as soon as people claim to know who I am, I can no longer act freely.

Someone in the group said that a whole lot of ghetto kids could have had a whole summer in the country for what this weekend cost. The black man quickly agreed. A tall blond girl blew up at him. She said that she wasn't in the least concerned about the money and that she couldn't care less about black, red, yellow, or white children. She said she was not there to solve the problems of the underprivileged and would like us to get back to the gut level of things. She accused the black man of cutting down white people simple because they weren't black, rather than admitting to the real sources of his anger. I felt threatened by her outburst. She had supported me earlier and I had responded warmly, but now I felt betrayed. Later when I told her about it, she said that, separated as I was by my wealth from most of the human race, I probably expected betrayal from everyone, especially women, whom I clearly did not understand. I said that I was surprised to hear her talk about understanding, which takes years to develop and occurs only when people feel free to expose themselves to one another. To even speak of understanding before then is a mockery, I told her.

When the group discussed prejudice, everyone became serious and apologetic. Finally I said, "Look, we're all very concerned about prejudice and we should be, but after all, there are only three black people in the group, whereas there are also several other people here who are victims of prejudice, and we aren't talking about their problems at all." At once attention centered completely on me. Whom did I mean? Were the men who administered my fortune prejudiced against me? When had anyone ever denied me anything? Then someone asked why all the talk was directed at me. One woman suggested that it was because I was articulate and had been overseas and was rich; I was clearly discriminated against because of my privileged status. Then they all began to analyze me. One person said I was obviously very strong, another that I was just as obviously sensitive, and another that I was masculine but soft. The black guy said that I frightened him, although he didn't know why. I asked them to stop giving me their bullshit and to attempt to get down to real emotions, not labels.

At the end of our encounter, one girl complained about my sarcasm. I said that it was just defensive humor, that I was sarcastic more to hide my bitterness than to alienate or frighten anyone. I said that living is an arbitrary matter; that every time I climbed a mountain in Nepal I expected to die on the way up or on the way down; that even now, whenever I drive anywhere, I don't expect to get where I'm going.

Taking part in the group has been important if only because it has taught me that no one possesses completely consistent emotions. In view of the discussions, I find that I can be described as neither a hostile nor a sympathetic person. Therefore, my sense of myself is entirely relative, and my hostility and sympathy vary depending on whom I'm with: I compete or I pity. Either I'm not good enough for anyone, or I'm too good for everyone. After this experience with the group, I want to give up contemplation and get out and move. Yet I am afraid that this energy is only a temporary reaction to my feeling of entrapment. Each time we met I became more aware of how dishonest all people are: we know our lives are chaotic, but we insist that everything happen in an orderly way, and that it be logically conceived.

Only two days ago we arrived here, perfect strangers to each other. In the adjoining parking lot we parked our respective Furies, Tempests, Escorts, Swingers, Barracudas, and Demons. Given the real nature of the destruction these cars bring upon us, they should all be renamed: Polluters, Colliders, Wasters, Annihilators, Autopsy-Coupes, Custom Disintegrators, and Maimers. Now, two days later, we are still strangers, anxious to return to our individual existences, and all the tears and hugs and screams and anger we manufactured seem vacuous and unreal. This concept of instant intimacy is what annoyed me most about the group encounter. The group seemed to break down resistances and make people feel good by allowing them to think that they were really getting to know one another. Yet nothing has happened; we know no more about ourselves and the others than we would after a cocktail party.

Here we are, I thought, a bunch of grown-up kids locked in an empty room playing naïve games with each other. No one understands anyone else. We are wandering around in dark caves, holding our private little candles, hoping for great illumination. But what if, because of my

past, I am more confused and limited than the others? Or
what if, for the same reason, I'm more complex and perceptive? In either instance, no one can help me find answers
to what I ask of life, least of all those who, fat with guilt,
treating their own life as a mere outline for some future
faultlessly plotted play, have become nothing but collectors
of their own sterility and inertia.

In the end I remain unfulfilled. I feel that I have not
confronted anything unknown. I told this to Karen when
I got back, and she accused me of unreasonably expecting
tangible results from the sessions. In fact, all I expected
was honesty.

The other day, on the giant screen of a Broadway
movie theater, I saw a film in which a number of people
were shot in the face. In one such scene a fountain of blood
bubbled up from a woman's mouth. In another scene a man
hit a woman with a bullwhip, then pressed his mouth to the
wound, then drew away with blood on his lips. Even though
I knew it was only red dye, I flinched. I tried to force
myself to stay and see the end of the film, but I couldn't:
I have had too many painful experiences. But what if my
past pain were nothing more than my own exaggerated
reactions to red dye?

Richard, one of my Yale psychology instructors,
learned from Karen that I was back in the country, and
yesterday we saw each other. Richard talked about our

society's treatment of the mentally ill as a yardstick of our humanity. He turned to a page in *American Notes* by Charles Dickens and quoted what Dickens had to say over a century ago about American insane asylums.

> The state hospital for the insane is admirably conducted. . . . At every meal, moral influence alone restrains the more violent among them from cutting the throats of the others; but the effect of that influence is reduced to an absolute certainty, and is found, even as a means of restraint, to say nothing of it as a means of cure, a hundred times more efficacious than all the straight-waistcoats, fetters, and hand-cuffs, that ignorance, prejudice, and cruelty have manufactured since the creation of the world.

During Dickens's time, the treatment of the mentally ill in America followed the lessons of Samuel Tuke, the British philanthropist and reformer. In Samuel Tuke's retreat the mad lived freely in their rooms, and as long as they did not violate the established codes of normal behavior and managed to restrain themselves, they were never punished or coerced. Thus, each patient was threatened only by the possibility of his own purposeful or inadvertent revelation of his madness to those around him, the patients and guardians alike. Once he realized that a madman's motives, thoughts, and emotions were of no interest to anyone, it was assumed that he would impose constant self-censure which would lead to his recovery.

But if by good behavior a madman could be turned so easily into a normal human being, couldn't any normal human being who doubted his own sanity be as easily turned into a madman? With such reasoning for a basis, the age of never-ending psychiatric therapy was upon us, and America was its retreat.

Recently, at a supermarket, Richard noticed the fruit and vegetable bins standing right next to the insecticides, bug repellents, and other household and garden poisons. He approached the manager, an older Jewish man, and told him that someone might spray the fresh food with poison. The manager was taken aback.

"Why would anyone want to poison the fruits?" he said in his heavy Eastern European accent. "What kind of a sick mind do you have that makes you think about such things!"

He started to move away, but Richard cornered him. "Why would anyone want to kill Jews?" Richard asked him. "Millions of your people went to the gas chambers, and you are no longer able to imagine one nut poisoning your fruit?"

Richard, a Jew, came to this country from the Ukraine after having survived the Nazi occupation there. He remembers losing everyone in his family on the day when the Nazis staged an elaborate outdoor execution of the local Jews—as well as the lunatics, the infectiously ill, and the badly deformed, who were all classified as racially impure.

Until the concentration camps and gas chambers became fully operational, the Nazis, like true showmen, often staged such outdoor events, and the local population and military units provided an attentive audience.

Such persuasive examples of punishment meted out in the name of law and order to those arbitrarily defined as different are part of our collective memory, and the slightest hint of nonconformity still somehow generates anxiety and fear in us.

In one revealing scientific experiment, Richard told me, several perfectly sane men and women were admitted to a mental hospital, where they were promptly judged mentally ill. In the same experiment, a substantial number of mentally ill persons applied for admission to a psychiatric clinic, and they were all thought to be perfectly sane. No wonder that two out of every five Americans are at some point diagnosed as suffering from psychiatric illness and are subsequently hospitalized. Half of all the hospital beds in the United States are occupied by psychiatric patients.

These relatively recent developments in our individual as well as our social and political behavior have prompted many psychiatrists to propose that the traditional categories of sanity and insanity no longer suffice. These psychiatrists claim that a new category—neither sane nor insane, but *un*sane—should be created for cases where environmental circumstances blur the difference between what is sane and insane—and modify assumptions and attitudes concerning sanity and insanity.

Even though health care is America's third-largest industry, millions of our mentally ill and retarded are excluded from most national health and medical-aid programs. These people live their lives unseen, routinely drugged, locked away in front of TV sets. Richard told me about one mental hospital where three thousand patients are attended to by no more than thirteen psychiatrists—a ratio of one to about every two hundred and forty. While so many of our mentally ill are left to suffer untreated, even unattended, innumerable normal men and women of our affluent middle class are being treated as mentally disturbed by gurus from some two hundred and fifty schools of psychotherapy, who often consider our natural anxieties as aberrational. Thus, psychoanalysis wants to cure neuroses through the interpretation of dreams, fantasies, and childhood memories; behavioral therapy aims at conquering phobias; cognitive therapy seeks to modify one's world view through logical reasoning; dynamically oriented psychotherapy claims to resolve the patient's unconscious conflicts through brief anxiety-provoking sessions; group therapy seminars enforce psychic discomfort as a means to self-management; integrated ther-

apy focuses on moment-to-moment experiences; hypno-
therapy induces a state of trance as a prelude to altering self-
awareness; and pharmacotherapy uses powerful psycho-
tropic drugs in an attempt to stabilize the pendulum of our
inner drives. Countless other therapies aim at stimulating
the patient's imagination, liberating his unconscious, or
increasing his energy by monitoring and manipulating his
bodily motions; still others use breathing, computers, and
even TV soap operas as means to calm down, restrain, and
cure the rebellious American psyche.

Often, Richard feels, the therapy itself creates a climate
of mental disturbance, anxiety, and maladjustment in patients by arbitrarily imposing on them mental, emotional,
and social straitjacket. As a result, each time the circumstances of ordinary life force them to display or define their
true identities, like the docile madmen in Samuel Tuke's
retreat these men and women become terrified by their own
inner or outer nonconformity and are no longer willing, or
even able, to pursue on their own who they are, to rejoice
in their spiritual uniqueness. I know what Richard is talking
about: I myself was once a docile madman.

I asked Karen what her life was like when I was away.
"I remember so many weekends, one just like the
next," she said. "At dinner, whatever man I was with would
help himself to the food first and talk too loudly. Then he
would suggest that I have champagne with him on his boat.
I would smile sweetly and say, 'Fine, but I'm not going
to bed with you.' I hate slick seduction scenes. In East
Hampton, I drank iced mint tea, ate sherbet, and smoked
hash. Finally, one summer, I ran into Sean, a handsome

son of a bitch whose teeth were so white they seemed to emit light. When Sean smiled, people put on their sunglasses. And everything else about him was just as perfect, just as beautiful—and I fell for that Moby Dick of the bedroom. I'm such a sucker for good looks—they symbolize life and health and love for me. Only in my erotic fantasies am I sodomized by vile old men who do to me what nobody else would dare.

"On the back of the photograph of himself that he gave me he wrote, 'Sean, age 27, no makeup, naturally perfect powermaster.' The naturally perfect powermaster had grown up in a shack in West Virginia. His family didn't have an indoor toilet until he was eighteen. At nineteen he left home, which broke his father's heart. When he was twenty-two he had an affair with a fifty-one-year-old nurse. There was nothing about healthy or unhealthy sex that she didn't know. She was a nympho and a swinger who liked it all, making up in bed for what she lacked otherwise, but eventually she wised up and decided to settle down with a well-to-do man who wanted to marry her. This left Sean with nobody to fuck or live with. Except, that is, his older sister, whom he liked a lot but who was married. He moved in with her and her husband, but after a week or so the sister's husband threw him out. According to Sean, the husband wanted to make it with him, but Sean refused to betray his sister. The truth was that Sean was too perfect to be just an ordinary heterosexual, and he hoped to draw the husband into an arrangement that would provide him with a home and meals, but the husband didn't fall for it. That left Sean on his own again, forced to rely on his good looks, even though he was convinced that it was his prick that helped him to survive.

"He once said to me, 'Let's face it. I may not be too smart, but I'm the best goddamn fuck this side of the Mississippi. My prick is above average, and in the sack so am

I.'" Then Karen got down to what she really wanted to tell me: "Not only his looks, but his direct approach really worked with me. I always want to give in when a man convinces me he'll do whatever he wants with me. I guess I don't like men who treat me with restraint. They make me feel slowed down, and then I blame myself for slowing them down. Just before you got back I had a date with a guy who was superliberated. He kept moaning about how sad it was that men depersonalize women and make them into playthings. Finally I couldn't stand it anymore. I told him, 'I can't help it if I don't turn you on. Just tell me if I don't, but if I do, for God's sake don't give me all this crap. Just take me to bed.'" She paused. "When you first went away, Jonathan, I wondered whether or not I should screw around and if I could actually get myself to do it. I knew I was vulnerable, so I tried to be cautious and rational. I'd heard about women getting fucked over by sex without love. After a few affairs, I tried to avoid having sex altogether because it drained me. I used to worry about being promiscuous, or becoming that poor moron of a woman I once portrayed in a medical advertisement captioned, 'Can a woman who's unhappy with one contraceptive find happiness with another?' How many men am I attracted to each year? Ten? Fifteen? Twenty? Eventually I might choose only three or four. When I'm attracted to a man, I say to myself: I like him, I desire him. I imagine getting laid, the touch of his skin and his muscles; I imagine breathing his breath and feeling him inside me. It's a straightforward desire, with no pretenses beforehand or regrets afterward. What could possibly stand in the way of it?"

When Karen spoke again her voice was low and husky. "Our knowing each other again, Jonathan, might lead to something good and solid, but I think it's too soon for me. I ended an intense relationship just before you got back. Things could still develop between us, but if they don't, at least we won't have deceived each other. We've always promised to be together only as long as it's good. I'm sick of my girl friends who suck guys off in parked cars or swing in groups of strangers because it's trendy. I'm tired of sexual fads."

She paused. "I like to do grass or take a downer, and I get stoned a lot," she said, "not only because it kills my inhibitions and makes me freer and funnier at a party, but because it opens me up sexually, lets me make a pass at any man I like; and it makes him braver with me. What's more, if things go wrong, I've something other than myself to blame it on.

"Last month I went through my first carefully planned threesome. After making reservations weeks in advance, we dressed in rented evening clothes of the thirties and went to the best restaurant in town. Janet was all glamour in her peach satin pants and top, I was in a gold lamé floor-length gown, and Robert wore white tie and tails. While ordering a super dinner—without drinks, wine, or champagne—each of us discreetly swallowed a downer. After coffee, all stoned, we staggered out of the dining room with the aid of our puzzled waiters and captain, who wondered how we had gotten ourselves so obviously sozzled. We went to Robert's apartment and had a wicked night of perverse but painless fun and frolic. In the morning, Janet rushed off to see her shrink. I had an assignment with a German photographer, and Robert dragged himself to his job at the travel agency. It's amazing what a good time I have when I can rid myself of that irksome brake known as conscience. Come to think of it, in order to enjoy that expensive food, we should have taken our downers after dinner! But seriously, for me sex is like walking in the hills. Each time you reach the top of one hill, you see another just ahead and you think that's the top, and then you see still another one, so you keep climbing, never knowing where the last one will be.

"I often have this nightmare. I hear a man's voice

coaxing and urging me, and I freeze and say, 'It isn't fair. You're taking advantage of me.' I feel like screaming, but then I think, what the hell, I'm a romantic cynic, I need it and I want it, so why not? Still, there are times when I can't come. It's emotional, I know, but what can I do about it? Sometimes when the sex is very good, I feel intense pleasure, but I'll never reach the highest hill." Karen got up and wandered around the room, talking on and on as if I weren't there.

"'You're the hottest lay I've ever had,' a man says, and I tense up and think he doesn't know what he's saying. Afterward, when he's no longer high and he repeats the line, I feel less afraid. 'Your body's built for sex and you know how to use it; most women just lie there and twitch. I can't believe you don't do it all the time. Tell me, has a guy ever come the minute he got inside you?' 'Of course,' I answer, still detached. 'I'm not surprised, not at all surprised. You've got the tightest box in the world.'

"In the kitchen, I'm mixing drinks and putting him on about his other women. He says, 'I know a good thing when I see it, and you're very, very good. With a body like that, you won't ever have to work an eight-hour day in an office.'

"After we make love, another man says, 'Fuck it, I'm not going to worry about being cool. I want to tell you it's never been this good for me. With you, it's like a whole orgy. You don't mind being told, do you?' 'Mind?' I say. 'I love it. Who needs that cool body-exchange swinging crap?'"

Karen looked at me pensively, then continued. "Truth is irresistible. It isn't a mistake to tell you this, is it, Jonathan? I tell myself that it's all right, that even if I don't love you enough, I can't stand your not loving me. Without your love I don't have any power over you. I can accept making it with a man I don't love—but not with one who doesn't love me. I'm terrified of being taken lightly."

Later that night she mentioned a letter I had sent her from Turkey. "You wrote that what excites a Turk most is to satiate his woman, to manipulate her body and mind, to enkindle her desire. Because Turkish men don't lose themselves in the women they love, they're supposed to be the best lovers. Why did you write me that?"

"The sect of lovers is distinct from all others; lovers have a religion and a faith all their own," wrote Indian thinker Jalal-uddin Rumi.

Even so, my impulse is not to respond when Karen says that I will continue to be an important but not an essential part of her life. By letting many men define her, she will avoid smothering and driving any one of us away. Her demand for attention is so great that no one man can fulfill it. Karen seems to choose men with the power to destroy her; unless she feels threatened, she becomes bored and leaves. She vacillates between seeing herself as predator and prey.

Karen is certain that her fantasies about sodomy with old men are no more terrifying to me than her fantasies of marrying me, having my child, and serving tea in the late afternoon are to her. She has often pointed out that my sense of myself is as fragile as hers: after each date both of us are sure we will never be able to see each other again. With Karen I try to remain cool, yet whenever she decides to hold something back from me, which is often, I find myself hounding her with questions, voicing objections, sulking, and falling into despair. Like her, I prefer to remain oblique, to avoid direct confrontation until a crisis—her open involvement with another man, for instance—compels me to define the true nature of my commitment. Meanwhile, each of us is going a separate way, and there is a danger that we will both lose by default. I keep recalling that ominous remark by Tolstoy: "Man survives earthquakes, epidemics, the horror of illness, and all the agonies of the spirit; but throughout all generations, the tragedy that has tormented him, and will torment him the most, is—and will be—the tragedy of the bedroom."

Living abroad, where my name did not win me instant acceptance, I was forced to see myself afresh. I noticed, for instance, that I avoided smiling because my smile exposed my unevenly shaped, irregularly set, and discolored teeth. I was reminded of that flaw again recently when Karen—whose own impeccably regular lips and faultless teeth are her professional trademark—studied my face and remarked that because I have beautiful eyes I should stare more at people, and smile less.

Through the company's medical research department, I thereupon met with one of the best dental surgeons in the country. I told him I wanted my teeth evened up and capped with a material that would make them look perfectly natural and, far more important, naturally perfect. After the surgeon had examined, X-rayed, and reexamined my mouth, he said that although he saw nothing wrong with my teeth, as long as I was troubled by their shape and color I should by all means have the work done. He then briefly outlined the

procedures, as well as the cost, for such extensive ortho-
dontic work, which he told me would take approximately
two months.

"Is there any way of having it done faster?" I asked.

"Well, yes. We could schedule more appointments per
week and speed up the lab work a bit," he said.

"I don't want to wait," I replied.

"How fast would you expect to have it all done?"

"How about in one day?"

Assuming I was joking, he chuckled politely.

"I'm serious," I said. "I want it done that fast, and
whatever the cost, I'll pay in advance."

Still uncertain, the doctor began to make calculations.
"I once capped all the teeth of a starlet in three days so she
could make her first movie," he said, glancing at the result
of his calculations. "I guess I could do it for you in a day."
He paused, still calculating. "I will cancel all other patients
and put everyone in the lab on alert. But I warn you," he
said, smiling mischievously, "after I'm finished with you,
you'll be much poorer."

"And you, much richer," I said. "When do we start?"

"Be in my office Monday at dawn," said the doctor,
reaching for the phone. "We'll try to have you out within
twenty-four hours."

Throughout the surgery, partly anesthetized, I would
catch the stare of the doctor and his attractive young nurse.
The two of them bent over me as if I were in an accident
and they were bystanders.

At one point I turned cold with fear, thinking, "What
if, through some unforeseen reaction to the anesthesia, I
were to die right now? Would the surgeon still have to cap

my teeth?" I even imagined the headlines: JAWS OF DEATH SNATCH INDUSTRY HEIR. VANITY KILLS AMERICAN SHEIK. "TOOTH FOR TOOTH" TURNS DEADLY FOR YOUNG MILLION-AIRE.

My father worked himself to death. At the peak of his career, his heart, unable to keep up with his unlimited drive to compete, stopped. Because my drive is limited, I could not even bring myself to go to war—the epitome of competition—since that would have unreasonably increased the chances of my death. My father's death seemed like destiny's corporate refusal to extend the loan of time he still needed to accomplish his task; my own would probably appear as an outright refusal to take out such a loan. Quite appropriately, Horace Sumner Whalen had been mourned by all who were in his debt. But if I, Jonathan James Whalen, were to die right now in my dentist's chair, no one would mourn the loss.

Between drillings, the doctor said to the nurse, "I'll give him another injection now," and through my filed-down teeth I mumbled, "I'm not 'him' yet, doctor. I haven't died."

While the lab technicians worked on my caps, I rested in the room adjoining the operating room. Groggy, my lips cracked, my gums in pain, I dozed. I kept thinking of the green-eyed nurse, of making a pass at her as soon as my new caps were installed, of carrying out with her a big seduction scene in some fancy nightclub and then fucking her in my hotel—all to erase from her memory the image of me as a pathetic-looking spike-toothed millionaire.

The next day I slept through lunch. When I awoke, feeling like an accomplice to a crime the dentist had committed on my body, I rushed to see myself in the mirror. The well-proportioned porcelain teeth looked as if they had always been there, but I immediately began to wonder how radically they changed my physical appearance. In the nineteenth century people assumed that white teeth free of decay indicated moral as well as physical health. What do such teeth signify today?

What next? I pondered. I recalled Barbara, who had thought my testicles were droopy and hung too low. Should I, I asked myself, go under the knife once more to improve the look of my testicles?

I called Karen. Luckily she was free to have dinner with me. In the evening I sent a car for her, and when she arrived at the restaurant I was already there waiting for her at a well-lighted table. As she walked toward me, escorted by the maitre d', men and women at other tables turned to watch her. Once again I realized that nothing I could do for Karen could match her own splendor.

She sat down, and as I ordered her favorite drink I felt her eyes on me. "You look so different, Jonathan," she said. I smiled, and she exclaimed, "Your teeth! What have you done to your teeth?" When I told her I'd had them capped, she said, "That's incredible. Now, when you smile, you look like Sean. You remember my telling you about Sean, don't you?"

While cashing a check for me, the night clerk at the hotel slipped me a handsome calling card inscribed: "2001 Love Odyssey: Elite Centerfold Residential Escort Specialists." Later that night I phoned 2001, and after a short introductory talk in which I sketched my ideal love mate, the madam said that my girl was on her way. The madam also let me know that money was a taboo breaker: in addition to the standard minimum, I might wish to pay the girl extra for what the madam called "Dr. Strangelove." The pun suggested bizarre lovemaking, kinky costumes, and role-switching.

The idea that I was about to make love to a woman—albeit a call girl—whom I had never seen and who had been selected for me by someone else I didn't know on the basis of my abstract description excited me more than any speculations I could possibly make about the girl concerning her age, her charms, or her skills.

The girl—my own private cheerleader—arrived on time. She was about twenty, fresh and pretty, the perfect model for a men's magazine centerfold or a TV soap commercial. I became instantly aroused by the prospect of doing anything I wanted with her.

"How much do you keep?"

"Half, plus the tip."

"This is for the night, then," I said, putting a number of large bills on the table in front of her. "And this is your tip."

"Do you always tip in advance?" she asked, not hiding how impressed she was by the tip, which was double the night's rate.

"I do. It encourages initiative," I replied.

"Then what's left for service?"

"Another tip—a reward," I said, hoisting up her skirt.

In bed, she behaved like a possessive steady girl friend, kissing and demanding to be kissed, insisting on being made love to. Each time I became engrossed in her immaculately clean, taut body, I was distracted by the thought of all the other men whose sperm, sweat, and spit must have filled her every pore and crevice.

After our lovemaking I asked her whether her shudders, moans, and orgasms were real or only a show staged for me.

"Why are you so worried about whether or not you were a good lay? Why should you care about the orgasms of an outcall escort?"

I told her I couldn't stand the idea of fucking a passive body, of letting myself be screwed and sucked by an anonymous piece of flesh with nipples and a vagina.

"Anonymous?" she shrieked. "You don't know what anonymous means. I was once a model, my friend; do you know what it's like to go down on a stinking garment district boss just to keep a lousy job? If only they'd say, 'We'll pay you five hundred dollars a week to fuck and blow us, and we'll let you be a star on the side.' But no, they want you to feel like a star so they can enjoy humiliating you each time you tongue their asses, lick them off, whip them on order. I'll tell you, in this city a woman needs two cunts: one for business and one for pleasure."

I began to think of Karen. Was there a time when, to get her first assignment, she too had gone down on someone? My silence put my cheerleader in a talking mood. She started to tell me her troubles, beginning with her first business blow job.

"The assistant to a television producer called me from Los Angeles and said he was going to fly to New York to meet me. He said I looked so perfect on paper that he wanted to see me in person. 'You could be the best in the business,' he told me, 'and I want to hire you, but what if you're too straight for my boss?' Later he called to say that he couldn't make it but that Maury, his boss, the producer himself, was arriving in New York that evening and

I should give him a call and have a drink with him. 'Baby,' the manager said, 'you can wrap this thing up. In one evening—with your sweet lips—you can wrap it up.' So that was it. All I had to do to get a television job with a producer was to go down on him.

"I saw the producer. We screwed. I went down on him. But straight sex was not what he wanted, and when I wouldn't do what he wanted me to do, he threw me out. I didn't get the TV job. Later, when I met his assistant, I played the outraged girl: 'Maury doesn't just screw,' I said. 'Maury is into leather and chains. I'm not.' The assistant was all smiles. He said Maury was going around telling everybody I gave him the best blow job he'd ever had. 'What a waste!' the assistant kept murmuring. 'Wasting that cream, all that cream, and not getting the job!' Then he decided that he himself wanted to be creamed. 'But how about me, kid? I'm into straight sex, and I can also help you out,' he said; 'no strings—chains—attached.' He leered, peeling down his zipper. I didn't want to touch him at first because I had my period and I hadn't washed; I felt uneasy even when he kissed my tits, but soon I really wanted to fuck him, maybe because I was accepted without having to wash. At first he couldn't get hard, and my choice was: either I help him—and I still might end up with a TV job—or I don't—and I wind up on welfare in a crummy one-room apartment, without even a TV of my own. The minute I made up my mind and went down on him, he managed to get it up. Then he gave me a whole load of crap about sexual, not just physical, love. The physical love, he explained, was like an emergency room: a quick release from discomfort was all you could hope for. But the sexual was a fancy clinic where you enjoyed all your senses. He turned me around and, gazing at my ass, said, 'The best thing about being honestly sexual is that, since our senses are centered in our faces, we must begin by looking. The lust of the eye is the essence of sex.' He could say this, that slurping worm, after I ate him with my eyes shut and my jaw aching, about to vomit from his smear.

"After that it was always the same, though not always as direct. First, sex was only hinted at. It began with: 'Take off your dress so I can see all of you. Pretend we've just met on a nudist beach. Don't worry, honey, I know how to control myself: I won't touch you, just eat you with my eyes. You don't have to do anything, just be your own beautiful self.' Then it was: 'You're so gorgeous! I love your smooth skin, your silky hair, your long legs, your round ass, your furry clit. You turn me on so much, baby doll, you could send me off just with your hand—or why don't you let me feel you inside? You're such a sensual kitten—I'll bet you turn on easily. Let's flood the little furnace.' Or else the guy would give instructions: 'It's the texture of your tongue and the way you flick it. Some girls just can't do it right. Now get it inside, as deep as you can, bite a bit, then kiss the rim. I said as deep as you can, baby, don't make me have to ask you again.'

"With a man thrashing under or above or in front of or behind me, on the couch, on the carpet, in bed, on the chair, on the john, at first all I could think about was whether I was doing it right. I worried about making a fool of myself. In this town everyone is whoring, so there's a lot of competition. It's not easy to be a good whore all the time with all the guys. Afterward I would cry, hating myself for even thinking about those guys. Still, I said words to them I thought they'd like to hear, words to make them feel like real men, words that depressed me more than fucking them. But these guys were all so stupid they couldn't tell the difference between a good honest lay and a bad one. I was willing to let them enjoy me, but why did they always do it wrong? Why did they have to abuse me? 'Can't you see my potential?' I'd say. 'I'm star material, you cockhead. Just look at me! I'm young, peach fresh, girlie soft, all willing, cheerful like a bird ready to take off. I want you to use my velvet skin, my lips, my tongue, my tasty cunt, my nice little ass. I want you to fuck me front or back so we can dig getting it on; I don't want to just follow your orders. Can't you see, you asshole, that when I do only what you tell me to do, it ends up being disgusting and degrading for us both?' "

I couldn't help thinking of Karen, and I asked her why she didn't quit.

"Quit for what? For office work? I can't even type a decent letter. I wouldn't last long as a fashion model; I eat and drink too much and get fat once in a while. In any case, these days models make it when they're thirteen. To be a private nurse? I have no patience with sick people. And I don't like to be alone for too long; I wallow and complain and don't do anything; I'm nowhere. I live only for suffering no pain, for looking good and keeping healthy. Everything I do I do to get a reaction from other people. I'm known now—maybe not in the way I wanted to be, but at least men notice me. They don't know who I am, but I look glamorous enough for them to imagine they've seen me on TV or in a magazine. From time to time I even enjoy being the way I am. I want money, and I don't really care where it comes from. Eventually I'll probably marry some rodeo rookie who'll think I'm all love and honey. Speaking about marriage and money: living and tipping the way you do, you must be rich enough to afford a wife with a rich past. Why don't you marry me?"

She woke me at dawn, and with the reward I had mentioned in mind, she made love to me with the zeal of a wife about to part with her beloved husband. After I rewarded her, generously, she assured me she would gladly fuck me for free, and then she left. I was drained of sperm and nagged by a single thought: if the whore had been diseased, I might infect Karen.

I told Karen that while I was abroad I sometimes came across photographs of her in American, British, German, and French magazines. I said I was surprised that she had so often consented to seminude modeling. Even now, I said, when men surround her in my presence, I can't help feeling uneasy knowing that so many of them have also seen her undressed—even if only in pictures.

"Have you ever known a woman who got old without being afraid of losing her looks?" Karen asked. "Have you ever known one who kept faith in herself? Thanks to modern medicine, we were supposed to have our youth extended well into old age. Instead, it all turns out the other way: we're terrified of aging, and we consider the old—even the middle-aged—inefficient, ugly, and repulsive. Look at the ages of Olympic athletes, or of models and stars today. They're kids.

"Sure I like to pose and be photographed that way— as naked and voluptuous as the law and the advertisers allow. Why not? My looks and my body are my defense against aging, the unavoidable law of nature. Beauty is my profession; and don't think I'm not terrified of being condemned to professional death by the faggots of the advertising business whose terror of age is matched only by their fear of the moral majority.

"Have you ever gotten 'prune fingers'—wrinkled fingertips after soaking a long time in a hot bath? One day all of me will be like that. Youth is the only commodity even you cannot buy for me. It's my nude photographs that reassure me—along with the advertisers—that I have nothing to worry about yet."

As a boy I would introduce my father to my friends by saying, "This is my father. He's a businessman. He's very rich. He owns everything." Instantly he or my mother would reprimand me for bragging. I deduced from their reaction that it was wrong for me to find my father powerful and rich; even if his power and wealth made him a fine and lovable figure to others, it was somehow wrong for me to love him for them.

During my years abroad, Karen befriended Susan, a college acquaintance of hers who worked in a New York advertising agency. On the surface, Susan is all Karen is not: ordinary, unobtrusive, modest, predictable. When Karen's professional career peaked and her income hit six figures, she told Susan that she could afford to hire a secretary to keep track of her appointments, expenses, and travel arrangements, and a housekeeper to cook and clean. When Susan volunteered to fill both jobs, Karen accepted. Susan quit her job and ever since has been a fixture in Karen's life.

Karen has been out of town, so today I took Susan to lunch. She reminisced about their college days. What she said casts a fascinating light on her own character and by implication illuminates Karen's notion of whom she should depend on. It also might explain why Susan has become Karen's most trusted ally, almost her Iago, ready to defend Karen against everyone—including me—and why I must be constantly wary of her.

Karen and Susan attended a women's college that seemed to turn out only girls who were well mannered, well groomed, and pleasant to talk to—perfect wives for doctors, lawyers, and businessmen. Susan told me that even though her college boyfriends could accept the fact that she was not a virgin, they were all preoccupied with and jealous of her previous lovers.

For almost two years Susan dated Christopher, a charming, handsome, brilliant scholar. She mentioned in passing two earlier affairs, and he thereafter assumed that she considered her first lover a mistake and her second merely a test case; he convinced himself that only now, with him as her lover, could Susan be sexually mature, aware of the flaws in her two previous relationships, and ready to settle down. Toward the end of their second year together Susan told him the truth: before she met him, she had had many lovers, women as well as men, even one-night stands. Stunned by her admission, Christopher called her a whore and refused to see her again.

Last year Susan found out that Christopher, by then an assistant professor of literature at a Midwestern university, was preparing to defend his doctoral dissertation on medieval passion plays.

She also learned that one of the most prominent authorities in the field of medieval theater was teaching at a New York university. Posing as a graduate student at that university, she obtained a passkey and entered the professor's office at night. The professor kept his notes neatly typed on small index cards in open files. Susan photographed all the cards containing pertinent research and theories and then returned the cards to the files.

At home she typed the material on various odd sheets of paper and envelopes. These she sent to Christopher along with a typewritten letter, which she assumed he would believe came from one of his ex-fellow students whose full name he could no longer even recall.

Dear Chris,

I remember that during our college years you were always interested in the theater of the medieval period. In case it's still your field, I enclose various notes on the subject left by my uncle, who died last week of lung cancer. Even though he was an advertising company executive, in his last few years he had become interested in passion plays. I'm sure he would be pleased to know that his research was not in vain, and that there is someone who can benefit from his—however amateurish—studies. All the very best,

Jim

After Christopher successfully defended his dissertation, it was filed in the university library. Susan then secured a copy and compared it with the material she had stolen. As she had hoped, Christopher had incorporated as his own a major portion of the information she had sent him.

Susan telephoned the New York professor and, pretending to be one of his past students, informed him that Christopher So-and-so, a recent doctoral candidate in the Midwest, may have plagiarized in his Ph.D. thesis certain ideas that she recalled from the professor's lectures. Soon after her call, the professor investigated the case and demanded a special inquiry at Christopher's university.

Christopher failed to explain satisfactorily how he had come into possession of the professor's materials. He could not even recall the name of the friend who, he claimed, had sent him the notes. He was dismissed from the university, and his academic career came to an abrupt end.

Volunteering her interpretation of my relationship with Karen, Susan remarked that it frequently benefited from my absence, when, like youthful masturbation, it could feed on fantasy. When distance separated us, Karen was forced to think about me, recall me, imagine me as her Byronic lover. As it was, Susan said, Karen and I saw each other only under "optimal conditions," that is, when we were both fit, in a good mood, anxious to be together. Susan meant to imply that because she shared a house with Karen, she alone had penetrated the spiritual as well as the physical sphere of Karen's selfhood.

Susan had indeed gotten to know Karen well. She had picked up Karen's mannerisms and idiosyncrasies of speech until it seemed that she was deliberately imitating her. At first she had also dressed as Karen dressed, copied Karen's hairstyle, taken up things that interested Karen, even went after men she knew Karen had been with. This continued until they became very close; then Susan grew self-confident enough to develop her own persona.

Karen once suggested that Susan and she and I live together, a possibility that involved no risks for Karen and Susan. I knew that Karen was not implying any three-part sexual relationship; still, I asked who would be the most expendable if our triad failed? Such an idea did not seem to have crossed Karen's mind. She will not admit to her dependence on Susan, and she would resent my describing their relationship in terms of dependence; but what is it the two of them share that I could not share with Karen alone?

Is Susan merely a receptacle for Karen's experiences, or does she mold them? I'm not convinced by Karen's explanation that Susan is a good companion, completely forgiving and patient. Such companions normally come and go. They meet other people, get married, have families of their own. But Susan is not seeing anyone else now; Karen is her life. I could give Karen financial security, but that's not what she wants from me, and I no more want to be Karen's servant than she wants me to become her benefactor. Sometimes I feel protective toward her, and of course I want her to be comfortable, but if our relationship is to develop, she must ultimately choose between Susan and me, between the very different attachments we represent.

I have no idea where I stand on Karen's list of emotional priorities, where I rank in relation to her work, to her pleasure trips, to her social life, or to Susan. Last week, to preserve her glamorous image in the society pages, Karen flew to Buenos Aires to be photographed with a bunch of local horse-breeding millionaires. Would she fly as far to preserve my image of her?

As the election nears, one of the local incumbent senators and his wife must have been reminded by their friends, the Howmets, that I am back in the country. My parents were always among the most generous of Republicans; with a little prompting I too might join and support the party.

I accepted the senator's invitation to attend a Fourth of July garden party at his Oyster Bay estate. The afternoon was to be enhanced by the presence of the vice-president, the governor, and other state and federal luminaries.

Because the senator's invitation was addressed to me

alone, Karen, upset that she had not been invited by name, refused to accompany me. I had to go alone.

The garden party was an elaborate affair, mixing food, drink, and dance with ad hoc tributes by film, stage, and TV stars. We were offered a political cocktail of well-prepared speeches by members of the senator's reelection committee, and there were a few inept utterances by some of his financial backers.

Delighted that I had arrived alone, Helen Howmet, who had taken her role as my godmother as seriously as if God Himself had appointed her, promptly introduced me to every rich and eligible debutante there. No doubt every one of them would have proved an unexceptionable wife for a clean-cut lieutenant of capitalist enterprise. But none of these girls matched Karen in looks or bearing; none of them interested me at all.

Exhausted by her matchmaking efforts, Helen Howmet finally left me alone, and as I mingled with the crowd I came across a familiar face: Keith Cushman, whose family owns The Cushman, a department store, and who, like me, was a failure at Yale and a draft dodger—another miserable exile from the American Dream. We first met in an Istanbul youth hostel. He was then immersed in making a career for himself in marine biology, and I remember still his childlike excitement over what he had learned about the jellyfish. That creature, after being fertilized sexually, begets a polyp. The polyp propagates asexually by budding, but it begets a sexually reproducing jellyfish; then the cycle begins again, the jellyfish always taking after its grandparents.

The sea squid was the other creature that fascinated Keith. During copulation the male squid blocks the female's breathing by inserting a sexual tentacle, one of its eight arms, into the female's cavity. Choked and fighting to break away, the female tears off the tentacle. While the severed tentacle remains inside of the female, the mutilated male swims away, to grow, in time, another tentacle in place of the missing one. The female later releases the tentacle, which starts a life of its own by becoming a sea serpent, a totally independent species.

I had also come across Keith in Amsterdam. He was then searching for another purpose, another label for his existence. He wanted to start a Marxist revolution in semantics, for he claimed that contemporary language had lost its ability to convey the spontaneous and could thus no longer serve as a meaningful revolutionary weapon.

Owing to a bad case of hepatitis, Keith had returned to America ahead of me. Now his health was restored, and he seemed glad to see me again. Drink in hand, talking in his usual dispirited, listless voice, he told me that while I was still bumming around abroad, he had married a young woman named Deborah, a City College graduate. However, he added, after two years of marriage, they were now divorced.

I asked how he had met her. He told me that she had been a contestant on *Blind Date,* a popular TV game show. In front of a live audience, she had had to select a date from among three bachelors who were hidden from her view behind a curtain.

From the moment she appeared on the screen, Keith knew that Deborah was the woman for him. In his travels, Keith said, he had been to a number of cathouses, and by the time he returned home he knew what it was in a woman that haunted his fantasies. He had also dated a lot, he said, and could recognize a woman perceptive enough to allow him to freely express himself sexually. On the show Deborah looked stunning; the questions she addressed to each bachelor were intelligent and witty, and her responses to their answers were effectively alluring. Even her final choice of Hugh—a rugged construction engineer from North Dakota—impressed Keith, despite his jealousy of that complete stranger who would now spend a week with as perfect a creature as Deborah.

At the end of the show the moderator announced the prize for Deborah and her date: an all-expense-paid idyllic week in Altos de Chavon, a newly built mountaintop retreat almost a thousand feet up, looking out over the green Chavon River on one side and the blue Caribbean on the other. As photographs of Altos de Chavon flashed on the TV screen, Keith speculated that he himself was no more a stranger to Deborah than was Hugh, whose only advantage was a brief conversational parrying with her during the program. Prompted by such thoughts, Keith decided to go after Deborah, the figure of his tele-fatuation.

On the day Deborah and her date moved into their suite in Altos de Chavon, Keith checked into the suite next door. When he spotted the couple having cocktails on a terrace above the Chavon River, he casually walked over and introduced himself as a fellow American. The *Blind Date* couple did not mind his intrusion; Deborah was almost grateful for it, for Hugh had little to offer in the way of conversation. Keith, an old hand in matters of politesse, was not about to make the life of the North Dakotan any easier. Keith quickly invited several other American guests—all accomplished writers, filmmakers, and artists who were visiting Altos de Chavon at the local government's invitation—to join them, first in conversation over drinks, then for dinner, and finally in a night canoe trip along the river to a picnic site on a moonlit Caribbean beach. Nor did Keith stop there: for the rest of the week, in a show of generosity toward Deborah, Hugh, and other "fellow Americans," he arranged fishing trips to nearby islands, parties at the oceanfront hotels of the Costasur, and trips to the museums and historical sights of Santo Domingo.

The week passed quickly. The dating game was soon over for Deborah and Hugh, who were about to depart.

Saddened, Deborah admitted to Keith that she was sorry to leave behind such a stimulating companion and that she looked forward to continuing their friendship in New York. Her obvious interest was not lost on Keith, and when the airport taxi pulled up and Hugh began to load their luggage into it, Keith told Deborah that he did not want to lose her, that he wanted her to stay—not just in Altos de Chavon, but in his life.

Soon after that, Keith and Deborah were married. The wedding was widely covered in the society pages, and the couple moved into a Fifth Avenue penthouse purchased by Keith's parents as a wedding gift. There Keith gave his bride a blank check, which she was to use to buy anything she wanted for herself and the apartment.

Because most of his friends, including me, were still living abroad, Keith said, during the marriage he tended to rely on Deborah's friends. The newlyweds entertained often, and before long Keith had met many people he considered far more interesting than anyone his parents or their friends had ever introduced him to.

"Why the divorce?" I asked.

"It wasn't my idea," said Keith with a touch of vehemence. "It happened without warning." And sensing my curiosity, he continued. "Even though Deborah and I smoked only pot, many of our friends liked uppers and downers, coke, LSD—you name it—and as good hosts we kept on hand a large supply of all that stuff. One night I had a headache and asked Deborah for a painkiller and a sleeping pill, which knocked me out. I was awakened by the voices of two uniformed police officers, who were taking notes as they listened to Deborah, standing before them in her nightgown. On the table lay my .45 caliber revolver and next to it several small packets of our hospitality stuff. 'What happened?' I asked, suspecting robbery.

"'While you got yourself high on that,' said one of the officers, pointing at the stash, 'you tried to kill your lady.' He directed his gaze at four bullet holes that hadn't been in the bedroom walls when I fell asleep. 'That's some fire power to use against a defenseless young lady,' said the other officer. 'You went quite out of control, Keith,' Deborah said, her voice soft, her expression full of innocent concern, 'and thank God you missed me before you conked out again. But I've decided to take no more chances with my life—or yours, Keith.' She looked at me with playful reproach. 'So I called the police.'

"Suddenly it dawned on me what had happened. Deborah wanted a child, and when she found out that, because of my faulty genes, any child of ours could be born with a birth defect, she decided to divorce me. She knew I loved her and would oppose a divorce, so she decided to set me up. Taking full advantage of the damaging evidence—I had no permit for the gun, not to mention the coke, hash, and other illegal mindblowers the police had found in my desk—Deborah filed for divorce. She won easily; the settlement—in which she got everything she asked for—was her private March of Dimes." He reflected. "Nietzsche claimed that everything about a woman is a riddle with one solution: pregnancy. But enough about Deborah," he said peevishly. "What about you, Jonathan? Are you still in love with that bionic beauty, Karen?"

For Karen, her brief, perishable relationships—the end of one already linked to the beginning of another—are proof of her freedom and of her victory over an ordinary existence; she refuses to do what her parents expect of her: to become, one day, a wife and a mother.

Because Karen is what I want, she holds the secret of who I am. Thus my relationship with her is, for me, a victory of self-knowledge over detached experience. But Karen, a living work of art, lives in time spans as short as those in which eye contact is made. Ceaselessly admired, a well-paid product of the industry of advertising, she cherishes her newly discovered independence. And so the two of us—she the Duchess of Independence, I the Duke of the Free—keep swearing to each other our love of freedom and independence. Even from and of each other.

Anthony was once my father's valet. I recently asked him to lunch. During the meal Anthony revealed to me why my father had fired him. One of Anthony's duties was to prepare my father's shaving cream every morning and, once a week, to insert a new blade in his razor. To prove his faith in the quality of products made of American steel, my father always insisted on shaving for seven straight days with the same American-made steel blade. Then one day Anthony overheard my mother complaining to my father that for the last three days he had not seemed smoothly shaved. From then on, without telling my father, Anthony put a new blade in the razor every other day.

One morning my father turned to him and said, "Yesterday I shaved with a blade that had a slight defect at one end. Still, it was a perfectly good blade, and it should serve me until the end of the week. What happened to it?"

"I changed the blade, Mr. Whalen," replied Anthony.

"What for?" asked my father.

"I thought you might need a fresh one," said Anthony.

"I do not," my father replied. "Bring back the old blade."

Under the scrutinizing gaze of my father, Anthony

admitted that he had thrown the blade away and that he had been changing the blades every other day for some time. When he finished speaking, my father turned to him and said calmly, "If that's what you think of our steel, Anthony, you needn't work for me anymore. My secretary will prepare your paycheck, and after you've packed, the car will take you to the station." Then, without another word to the man who for years had served him like a faithful dog, my father returned to his shaving.

Anthony also told me valuable truths he had learned from my father, who in the good old times would chat with him while shaving. On the day my father learned that General Motors had begun to manufacture its Corvette Sting Ray—a limited-appeal, very expensive fiberglass sports car—he promptly summoned a meeting of the board of directors of his company. He told them that every twenty-four hours, ten thousand new drivers and just as many new cars are added to our roads; that the American consumer spends one out of every four dollars on the automobile; that car production consumes twenty percent of our steel. What would become of the steel industry, the backbone of our economy, he asked, if all American cars were to be made of fiberglass? Regardless of the small market envisaged by Detroit for the two-seat Sting Ray, his company would no longer sell steel on preferential terms to General Motors. Soon after, having spotted the wife of a top-ranking Chrysler executive driving a Japanese-made compact, my father telephoned her husband to inquire why he let her do it. Annoyed, the executive replied that his wife was a free citizen—free to drive any damn car she chose; and promptly my father ceased doing business with Chrysler. That meant he was preferentially supplying steel only to Ford and Studebaker. Some years later, however, when Studebaker announced production of the Avanti, its five-seat mass-market fiberglass sedan, my father blew up, called the move blackmail, withdrew his product, and swore that Studebaker would pay dearly for their desertion of the steel industry. Indeed, Studebaker soon faced serious financial difficulties and, on the verge of bankruptcy, ceased its car production in the United States.

"Have you decided what you're going to do with yourself, Jonathan?" Anthony asked me. "Are you going into business? You're still young, and it would be a real pity to waste yourself doing nothing—or doing the wrong thing."

Anthony seemed to think that my present life, like my years of draft dodging and drugs, was nothing but evasion of responsibility. I changed the subject, chatted about my travels, said how much I had learned from my exile. Anthony remarked that I was lucky to have so much freedom—meaning money. When I tried to tell him that money could not buy the inner freedom I have always desired, he wasn't interested. When he said how much I resembled my father, I became angry. I wanted to tell him that was a lie, as he of all people—a black man, the archetypical American servant—should know. But I checked myself. I started instead to talk about some of the women I had had, asking him pointed questions about his own sex life and telling him increasingly realistic stories. He laughed at first, but as the episodes became more lewd and violent, he began to grow uncomfortable, and exhausted by the thought of even the possibility of such adventures, he slumped in his chair. I don't know why, but perversely I continued until I was sure he realized that my life was beyond his experience.

A penthouse tenant of my hotel called the police about something she saw from her balcony: a man attempting to cross the East River Drive on foot in the midst of the evening rush hour was struck by a car that did not stop after it hit him. It took the police thirty minutes to arrive at the spot, and by then the dead body was flattened. Car after car had run over it; not a single one had attempted to slow down or stop.

I wonder if it ever occurred to my father that, whether the automobile was made of fiberglass or steel, more Americans have died in automobile accidents than in all the wars our country has fought in the last two centuries. Or that in fifty-three American cities highways occupy a third of all the land; that half of the land of Chicago, Detroit, and Minneapolis is given over to traffic and parking lots. My father, a clear-thinking businessman and industrialist, must have been aware that the societal cost in loss of life and property caused by car accidents was ten times higher than that caused by all other crime and violence combined. And if he was aware and did not speak up against such destruction, then was he guided—or corrupted—by his lust for profit?

The less you *are*, the less you give expression to your life, the more you *have*, the greater is your *alienated* life and the more you store up of your estranged life. Everything which the political economist takes from you in terms of life and humanity, he restores to you in the form of *money* and *wealth*, and everything which you are unable to do, your money can do for you: it can eat, drink, go dancing, go to the theater, it can appropriate art, learning, historical curiosities, political power, it can travel, it is *capable* of doing all those things for you; it can buy everything; it is genuine *wealth*, genuine *ability*. But for all that, it only *likes* to create itself, to buy itself, for after all everything else is its servant. And when I have the master I have the servant, and I have no need of his servant. So all passions and all activity are lost in *greed*.

So says Karl Marx.

Have I reached a spiritual stalemate? Am I estranged from life? Do I, even with my income, need to work, just like the masses who commute daily on the subway or drive their cars for hours to and from grueling eight-hour jobs? Or am I to enter into competition with the captains of industry, who still work at increasing their power and wealth?

Why should I? My capital, invested and reinvested by my brokers, increases on its own so fast that nothing I could do would possibly add appreciably to it.

And finally, why should I feel ill at ease about enjoying the wealth that came to me legitimately, that originated in the hard work of hundreds of thousands of people and now benefits thousands of other people who, thanks to it, are employed and productive? Why should I lead a miser's existence on a millionaire's income?

Had I had a talent, it would define me as writer, composer, painter, or sculptor and carve out a place for me in society. But talent is one commodity that even I cannot buy. My only recourse, then, is finding a spontaneous, natural activity that will allow me to know myself and others—and do harm to no one.

Well, I've found one.

The immediate, natural, necessary relation of human being to human being is the *relationship* of *man* to *woman*. . . .Therefore, this relationship *reveals* in a *sensuous* form, reduced to an *observable* fact, the extent to which the human essence has become nature for man or nature has become the human essence.

I could have written it, but I did not. Karl Marx did.

Karen speaks fondly of Amsterdam and loves her modeling assignments there. She says it is an ultimately civilized city, where she doesn't have to make many adjustments, where almost everyone speaks English, and where nobody cares if she sleeps with a man, a woman, or both at the same time. True Protestants at heart, the Dutch relegated sex to the realm of either a marital duty or a tourist diversion, saw it as just one of life's many surfaces, and by doing so effectively dismissed any power it might have as a threatening obsession.

Karen's response to Susan is much the same: Susan is familiar, undemanding, easy, and—with Karen—acts spontaneously. They respond to each other's needs, even when those needs are inconvenient or come at inconvenient times. Yet, I suspect, even with Susan, Karen does not reveal everything, and if at times they're lovers, Karen remains sexually ambiguous—and uncommitted.

In spite of the libidinous poses Karen strikes in her ads and fashion photographs, her obsessive sexuality does not find expression in her letters to me, even in the poems she occasionally writes. For all of her sexual experimentation

with men, women, and couples, and her spontaneous—
though often pot-induced—bed-hopping, I suspect that with
me she is still sexually mute, unable to give voice to her
many urges. I suggested to her that she might consider
writing intimate letters to me in the third person, just as in
her modeling she is often asked to portray someone else.
This would give her the freedom to have her desires and
thoughts, however outlandish and incriminating, attributed
to her protagonist, a freedom enjoyed by storytellers and
novelists down through the centuries. The idea had never
occurred to her.

After having lunch with two of my former trustees, I
went back to my hotel and began to telephone some friends
whose names and numbers I found in my old address book,
but I couldn't reach any of them. Everyone must have
moved while I was away. Just as well. Unlike Karen, who
likes to hang on the phone for hours, I hate it. Talking on
the phone is yet another substitute for real intimacy; a bit
like looking at someone's picture instead of being with the
real person. When I called Karen I got no answer, so after
a few drinks I called again. This time she answered. She
sounded somewhat drunk, and I could hear Susan's voice
in the background. Karen giggled and chattered, and imagining her and Susan making love, I started to masturbate
but couldn't come. I took a Somaphren, dozed off, and
awoke in the middle of the night, wanting to be with someone—anyone. I thought of inviting the hall porter for a
drink, then of calling the 2001 for a girl, but, feeling groggy,
I wasn't certain whether I was in the mood for either one.
Through it all, an inquisitive voice kept saying: What if this

is insanity? What happens next? What if only I know of my condition while others continue to assume I am normal and healthy? If whatever I think is distorted by my illness, how can I, a mentally ill person, help myself?

I took some more Somaphrens, fell asleep again, and dreamed of my mother. I saw her alone, having one of her attacks, scurrying from one corner of her bedroom to another, searching like a panicky thief for the drugs that she had hidden from her nurse. She was looking under the bedside tablecloth, in her bed, inside the drapes, among the books and magazines. Before the nurse appeared, my mother had swallowed several pills. Then, telling the nurse that she wanted to pick out a book, she ran downstairs to the bar next to the library and gulped from a half-empty Scotch bottle. She rushed back upstairs, turned on the TV, and went to bed. As the drugs and alcohol stifled her anguish, she drifted into sleep under the watchful eye of the nurse.

There was no feeling of the presence of death at my father's funeral. Instead, there were speeches, banks of flowers, long lines of cars with their headlights on, photographers, television cameras, crowds of people standing under black umbrellas in the rain, and a police helicopter hovering discreetly above the cemetery. That was all. I never saw my father's corpse. I would like to make up for that now by imagining my mother's death.

When I am depressed, doubt infects my emotions and despair corrodes my intellect. Unlike my natural drives for sex, sleep, and food, my depression arises from my failure to arm myself morally, spiritually, and philosophically against such doubt and despair. I could as easily have done something else yesterday afternoon, but in order to dull my mind I chose to be depressed, that is, to enact again a familiar ritual. Reenacting ritual in this way makes me feel as though I were in control of my depression rather than the other way around: the ritual makes the depression seem premeditated, and its mood, however painful, almost calculated and predictable.

Karen and I went to the Manhattan Transfer Theater on Broadway to see the recent theatrical adaptation of Theodore Dreiser's *The Financier*. During the intermission, many theatergoers recognized Karen. Men and women, old and young, in everything from evening clothes to work shirts and jeans, came up to her, complimenting her on "being herself," on "looking great in that jeans commercial," or telling her, "I saw your picture on TV, didn't I?" "You are someone famous, aren't you?" "You're the best-looking American girl ever." These well-meaning people treated Karen as if she were a stage or screen actress and as if her good looks were the result of a rare dramatic talent that she had developed through her own hard work.

Predictably, men were Karen's most eager fans. Seductively looking into her eyes, one after another they came to pay her tribute, murmuring, whining, or whispering such profundities as "You're even more beautiful than your TV commercials"; "You are every man's dream come true"; "After seeing you I'll hate my girl friend"; "You're too beautiful to be real"; "Can I kill somebody for you?" While Karen accepted their tributes with grace and charm and a made-to-order, sincerely offered "Thank you so much," I found myself becoming irritated and jealous. Didn't these hillbillies of American seduction, these delicatessen Lotharios realize that, if indeed Karen was as great as they thought, she would most certainly by now have picked out the man of her choice? Or several men? And what about me? Who did they think I was? What did they think I was doing sitting there beside her with her hand in my lap?

I read in the program that Theodore Dreiser, in *A Book about Myself,* admitted that he had settled in New York to become rich and famous. In New York, he said, "everything was in the making: fortunes, art, social and commercial life. The most impressive things were its rich men, their houses, factories, clubs, office buildings, and institutions of commerce and pleasure." According to critics and scholars, the character of Frank Cowperwood, the protagonist of *The Financier,* was based on the life of Charles Yerkes, the American streetcar baron and Dreiser's contemporary. Yerkes was suave, handsome, a scholar and sybarite who was an art collector as well as a lover of some of the most glamorous women of his day. Dreiser, who desired notoriety, comfort, and personal freedom, found Yerkes's image appealing. Like Yerkes, Dreiser was a sexual adventurer; at one time in his middle age he maintained a liaison with a girl of seventeen. Moreover, Dreiser realized that he and Yerkes were both social inventors who designed large schemes for others to follow—Yerkes in finance and industry, Dreiser in his novels.

In his *Maxims of Happiness,* Charles Yerkes had a few things to say about acquiring wealth, among them: "Wealth does not buy happiness; it buys luxuries" and "It is love of wealth that can never be gained that makes men unhappy and often drives them to wrongdoing. We cannot all be millionaires." Even Charles Yerkes had no advice to give, however, to those of us who were born millionaires.

As I read about Dreiser's life and his fascination with

money, power, and Charles Yerkes, whose life he used as a model for all three novels of his "trilogy of desire," I wondered whether, had Theodore Dreiser ever married my widowed mother, he would have been able to present the true, convincing, and dramatic portrait of one Jonathan James Whalen, his millionaire stepson.

Later Karen and I had a meal at the Babbitt, the fancy new Arab supper club, where tuxedo-clad, foreign-mannered, money-scented smoothies tried their number on her, smiling and whispering compliments as we passed by them. Even after we sat down at our table, they still kept staring at her.

One of them was particularly persistent. He was unnaturally obese; layers of fat swelled his cheeks and chin, rolled round his neck, fell like a mantle over his shoulders and arms. He was seated at the head of a table where four or five couples—I gathered by their toasts—were celebrating his birthday. Yet from the moment this glutton saw Karen, he became almost as transfixed by her as he was by his food. He dropped his gaze only when occupied with another large piece of meat, more potatoes, a helping of salad, a slice of cheese, and a large portion of the birthday cake—all of which he swallowed with unending greed.

I summoned the maitre d', and discreetly pointing out the glutton, I ordered the restaurant's richest chocolate cake and asked the maitre d' to send it to his table and put it on my bill. Within minutes the waiter delivered the cake, indicating that it was a gift from me. Accustomed to my little pranks, Karen was amused.

The glutton was enchanted. As his table companions

turned to look at me, the anonymous benefactor, the glutton waved his thanks. Delighted with a new opportunity to indulge, he began to devour great chunks of the cake while his friends and Karen watched.

When he had finished the last bite, the glutton heaved himself from his chair and steered his huge trunk through the dining room to our table. "That was mighty gracious of you and your sweet lady," he said to me, his eyes on Karen. "Mighty gracious." Then, turning toward Karen, his great belly almost hiding her from my view, he said, "I sure could eat up your sweet little lady here, just like I ate that cake!"

I patted him on his shoulder. "You still haven't asked me why I sent you the cake," I said, all charm.

The glutton turned toward me. "Why did you?" he asked, puzzled.

"A scourge of folly," I said. "I knew you couldn't have your cake and eat it too." I smiled at him sweetly and added, "Then, too, there was the tempting chance that one more mouthful of food would kill you—right in front of me and my sweet little lady!"

When I was a boy, my father used to drive me through the countryside on the outskirts of Pittsburgh. While he worked the clutch of the car, I was allowed to sit next to him and work the gearshift. One afternoon we passed two men in hunting caps and leather jackets running along the highway with rifles in their hands. When we heard shots, my father stopped the car, and soon the hunters appeared, dragging a dead deer. Although I was fascinated by the thought of hunting down an animal so well equipped that it could outrun and outsmart a man, my father was horrified by what we saw. By giving in to the base pleasure of killing creatures so much weaker than themselves, he said, men turned into spiritual Nazis, who could eventually lose respect for even the lives of humans they considered inferior.

I told Karen that whenever I make love to a woman who is menstruating, the sight of her blood and the pungent, natural vaginal scent make me sexually more active, almost aggressive, which might be an atavistic throwback.

I once went to bed with a girl who, even though she was suffering from a yeast infection, was unwilling to cure herself with drugs or medicated douches because she believed they would irrevocably alter her body's natural functions. We were both naked, kissing and caressing, but her fetid odor made me unable to get excited. The girl began to worry about my failure to have an erection, and instead of pretending I had a headache or some such thing, I told her the truth and suggested that she douche or insert a scented suppository. The girl then accused me of being insensitive and of treating her like a whore. Further argument was pointless, so we parted enemies.

"I love to have my period," Karen announced. "The steady pull of blood makes me feel like nature's donor. I hate birth control pills because they reduce my flow. I prefer to play Vatican roulette—the calendar rhythm method.

"No healthy being should prefer the flavor and taste of synthetics—raspberry, jasmine, orange blossom, or champagne douches to the piquancy of the body's own secretions." Mustering her arguments, she paused, then continued. "They force us to take the pill, to insert IUDs, to douche, to depilate our bodies, to be manicured and pedicured and cured of smells they don't like. They might succeed in penetrating our brains as well as our vaginas—but they will never understand our biology." She did not say who "they" were, but she succeeded in reminding me that as a man I am forever prevented from comprehending what makes a woman a woman.

I showed Karen some men's magazines and tabloids filled with sex-for-a-fee ads, most of which contained semi-nude or nude photographs of beautiful, shapely young women along with phone numbers. The ads read: "Sandra, an actress between engagements, will engage you in her act." "Norma has a touch of class. Enjoy the class of her touch." "Her father hates Georgina for what she's doing. You'll love her for it." "Rona, her master's toy; spank me, whip me, tie me up." "I'm eighteen, tall, deep-throated, plenty of tits, ass, and legs for you to play with. Come to me and I'll make you come. Yours, Bettina." "Yolanda—angelic beauty, beastly lust. Purity you'll like to soil." "Paying for your girl friend when going out? Why not pay me, the dream girl you can go in with?" "I'm Tara. You saw me in fancy fashion ads—fancy loving me, any fash-ion."

"It's so much easier for a man to ask for, and get, the sex he wants," said Karen in response to this display of flesh for sale. "You can call any of these women up, treat her like a lady, pay her to enact your fantasy for you, and afterward feel no remorse. Fucking a whore has been a man's right for centuries. But if I were to hire a gigolo for a night, I would feel like a defenseless junkie entertaining an escaped convict."

She began to reminisce. When she was a six-year-old playing with other kids, she said, she began to seek sexual pleasure by rubbing herself against the pole of a slide or by pressing her body against the rough canvas of the porch hammock. Her masturbation was instinctive from the start; she never had to be taught how to please herself, and as her sexual needs increased, she discovered that by prolonging self-stimulation she could conjure up sexually exciting images of herself with others and finally reach a climax that broke her tension and calmed her down.

"As a young girl, making love with you, Jonathan," Karen said, "I had already discovered that if you were quick and violent and deep inside me, I would come only once, as fast as you, breathlessly and disheveled, but from the very depth of me. By myself, or with a man—or woman—bent on foreplay and kissing, I can climax on and off for hours, but I never lose control of myself." She paused. "I've been conditioned to take my pleasure only from pleasing others. When a man asks me how he can make it good for me, what I want him to do to me, or how I see him in my fantasy, I get a mental cramp and can't tell him. After all these years, I'm still not brave enough or abandoned enough to use a man for my pleasure, or even to satisfy myself as he watches—one of my biggest turn-ons in fantasy. To please a man, I usually fake my orgasm, and while I may be repulsed by my own cowardice, I despise him more for abetting my fakery."

Recently Susan was out of town, and Karen went to a movie with a married couple she knew casually. Afterward she invited them to her apartment for a drink.

Left alone with Karen for a moment, the wife, a shy, stolid woman with a willowy figure, innocently confided to Karen that her marriage was threatened: her husband had told her that he slept with other women during his business trips away from home and that on occasion he went alone or with a woman to swinging clubs.

Over drinks the husband, a jovial, well-built man, jokingly made passes at both Karen and his wife. Then he asked Karen whether he and his wife could make love in one of the bedrooms, and Karen coolly offered them Susan's room. When Karen was about to leave them there, the wife gently embraced her, saying, "Stay with us. We're free-minded." Karen hesitated. "Yes, please, join us," said the husband, seconding the wife. "You don't have to do anything; we don't mind being watched." Curious to know her own reaction to being in bed with people she hardly knew, Karen consented. They all undressed and a bit clumsily crawled into Susan's double bed. The couple started to fondle each other, and then Karen became aroused by the sight of the wife being forcefully taken by her husband. When, from under her husband's bulk, the wife reached out her hand, searching first for Karen's breasts, then sliding down, Karen gave in to her own need and kissed the woman on the mouth, then on the nipples and belly, then forced herself between the man and the woman. Encouraged by his wife and Karen's excitement, the husband started to stroke Karen's thigh; then, with her quiet consent, gently impaled her, then alternated in his thrusting between Karen and his wife as the two women lay absorbed in him and each other. All through the night the initiative seemed to spring from the wife, and eventually Karen became aware that the woman had a marital plot: by bringing about Karen's seduction, she sought to become a necessary partner to her husband's need.

As I listened to Karen's clinical account of the incident—by her own admission, only one of several such incidents—I wondered: was I, as her lover, chosen by her to be the one from whom she had no secrets, or was I simply another lover?

I received a note from Helen Howmet: "Dear Jonathan, In case you haven't seen it yet, the enclosed article might interest you. Love to you, Helen."

The article was a feature story from a Manhattan-based society weekly, and it claimed that Cyrus Rawleigh, "the youthful Texan who owns Rawleigh Gas and Oil," and Karen, "a top-paid U.S. cover girl," had become "on-and-off" globe-trotters, enjoying each other in chic resorts as well as on secluded islands. Accompanying photographs showed Karen and Cyrus Rawleigh dancing in Saint-Tropez, tanning themselves on the Rawleigh yacht in the Bahamas, and lounging cozily on the patio of his San Antonio ranch house.

At a time when the gossip sheets list single models and actresses along with heiresses and women executives as the nation's most eligible bachelorettes, Karen has been a consistent front-runner in the matrimonial sweepstakes conducted by society editors. Described often as an "all-around certified beauty," and "the perfect companion for the man who has everything," this year she was also selected by all the major gossip columnists to be the newest member of their Eligibility Hall of Fame.

When asked why her name is most often linked only with those of millionaires, Karen supposedly answered, "Maybe because they make me determined to remain independent, career-oriented, and sane enough to be self-centered." By now I had learned to take all such verbal crap with a large dose of salt. However, looking at the pictures of Karen with Rawleigh, I was alarmed by her pose: it was the pose of a woman in love.

I called Karen, and Susan answered. Before calling Karen to the phone, Susan warned me that Karen had just returned from assignments in Alaska and Brazil and was tired and suffering from a throat infection.

Karen sounded friendly. She was anxious to see me, she said, and to have the two of us spend some time together. Filtering any emotion from my voice, I said I would like that very much and that I hoped I could make her as comfortable as she seemed to have been with Cyrus Rawleigh. She was silent for a moment; then she said a bit brusquely that Cyrus was her old and trusted friend. She was indeed comfortable with him, she said, because to Cyrus she was the whole world, not just another bridge to it. As an afterthought, she mentioned that in a week or so she and Cyrus planned to spend a few days in the Canadian Laurentians, where rest and the high altitude should clear up her throat infection. She talked lightly about her forthcoming assignments, the film she was doing, and a Maryland horse-breeding farm she had considered buying as an investment and a means of lowering her taxes. Then, without mentioning Cyrus again, she promised to call me soon and we hung up.

My first impulse was one of jealousy, which soon gave way to conflicting thoughts. What was it I objected to? That she might have fallen in love with another man? But falling in love was her right. That she didn't tell me about him? Why should she? Was I her lover-confessor? What was it I wanted from her anyway? A weekly mailing of her thoughts? A subscription to her moods? A ticker tape of her sex life?

Determined to calm down, I turned on the TV. Switching from channel to channel, I saw Karen's famous American champagne ad twice in less than an hour. As her smile and hips flashed wetly across the television screen—the pictorial landscape of America—I thought of Cyrus Rawleigh. Did he believe he was the sole owner of Karen's smile and hips?

After Karen's commercial, Louise Hunter, a young Broadway actress I recalled in *The Financier*, was interviewed about the prospects for a settlement of the two-month-long actors' strike. She was flawlessly beautiful, with a lean, smooth, sinewy body. As I listened to her tell how the strike had threatened her financial security, as well as that of her actor-husband, I realized what I ought to do. I telephoned one of the secretaries at the company and asked her to invite Miss Hunter to dine with me to discuss her availability for a dramatic assignment.

The secretary arranged for dinner the following evening at the American Mercury, America's most expensive restaurant.

As the maitre d' guided Louise Hunter to my table, I noted that she was surprised by my appearance. "With your references, Mr. Whalen, I thought you would be an old corporate goat who wanted to invest in a play—or an actress—for some special reason." She spoke with the ease and charm of the professionally gifted.

"You were right, Miss Hunter. I want to invest in a very special play, and I want you to be its star," I said as I took her soft, narrow hand.

"I'm flattered; tell me more," she said, smiling politely. We ordered drinks and looked at each other shyly.

"It's the story of a man," I said. "A young American plutocrat. His mistress, a famous American fashion model courted and admired by many wealthy and powerful men, does not fully reciprocate his love.

"One day he hires a young and beautiful Broadway actress to accompany him on a three-day sight-seeing trip to London, during which her sole task is to pretend that they have just fallen madly in love and are in London to hide from the world—as well as from her jealous husband

and the plutocrat's mistress. While the plutocrat and the actress dine out, dance, see the sights, and enjoy each other in their hotel, they are followed by dozens of photographers and gossip writers who have been hired by the plutocrat. When the story of their liaison hits the society pages of all the American newspapers, the plutocrat's mistress realizes that she is not his only love and becomes jealous. That makes for a perfect ending, because arousing her jealousy was the purpose of the trip."

"Interesting," said Louise Hunter. "Will this be a theater piece or a movie?"

"Neither," I answered.

The captain, wine steward, and waiters were hovering around us, and I sensed her growing curiosity.

"What will it be, then?" she asked.

"A happening," I said calmly. "A real-life psychodrama, financed by me, in which I will be the plutocrat and you will be the actress."

"Do you know, I was stupid enough to think you were serious," said Louise Hunter, visibly disappointed.

"I'm in love with a woman—a fashion model—who is not possessive enough about me," I said. "Your provoking her jealousy is very serious to me—"

"But not to me," she broke in. "It's a rather unattractive role." Her manner was chilly and defiant.

"Maybe so," I agreed. "But it is about love, and as Yeats says, 'Love has pitched his mansion in / The place of excrement: / For nothing can be sole, or whole / That has not been rent.' In any case, if you decide to go through with it, for your three days in London you'll be paid as much as you probably made in three months in *The Financier*."

"But why me?" she burst out. "There are so many professional escorts!"

"You're well known: these days, to make the gossip

columns, one has to be more than simply rich. You have talent; all I have is money."

Leaning closer, she looked at me anxiously. "But all this publicity will make everyone think that you and I really *have* been lovers. What then? What about Frank, my husband?"

"Tell him you're going with me to London on a publicity stunt, to portray a mistress—not to become one! The two of you are actors; publicity is the stuff of your life; and this trip will put you smack in the public eye! Why should he object to that? It's the truth."

Lowering her eyes, Louise Hunter demurely pondered what I had said. "There are a few plays I would enjoy seeing in London," she said.

"Then we will see them together," I said as the waiter poured more champagne.

To save our energy and make our trip to London more comfortable, I had six seats reserved, three in each row, to be used as beds during the flight. I had learned this trick from my mother, who also always traveled with a basket containing a meal prepared by our French chef. The plane was crowded, and the other passengers, as well as the stewardesses, glanced with obvious scorn at Louise and me sprawled in our private cribs. At one point, accosting me in the aisle, a woman asked me with sarcasm, "What makes you beautiful people so special?"

"Chance injustice," I answered. "My girl friend's beauty is her inheritance; my inheritance is my beauty."

The public relations company I hired had suggested that Louise Hunter, not I, should become the bait for the

British and American press. Through her, they'd assured me, the media would eventually zero in on me.

At Heathrow Airport Louise was photographed and interviewed for British TV and several newspapers and magazines. In the hotel, where we purposely occupied separate but neighboring suites, to maintain the pretext of secrecy, she refused to see the press. However, well alerted by this time to our presence, British photographers trailed our car our whole first day in the city, and we let them catch us at various points. The press particularly enjoyed photographing Louise during our dinner at the Baobab, and later at the Cockpit, a fashionable disco where Louise appeared in a dress that bared more than it covered.

When we danced, I was aroused by the sight of her breasts, by her mouth next to my earlobe, by the brushing of our hips, and I reached for her as if she were my lover. Instantly her manner reminded me that I was asking for more than our bargain called for.

Throughout our London psychodrama, as we held hands, embraced, kissed, and looked into each other's eyes for the sake of the photographers, the conspiratorial camaraderie Louise assumed helped me to behave as if I were passionately in love with her.

She told me that her husband had proven more understanding of the nature of her assignment than she had expected and that she didn't think any amount of publicity and gossip about the two of us would change his attitude.

The first mentions of our escapade, accompanied by photographs, began to appear in the New York tabloids two or three days after our return. These were followed by longer, equally gossipy pieces in the media weeklies, and eventually the "people" sections of national magazines picked up the story.

In most of these items Louise was called "the Broadway starlet of *The Financier*"; I was variously described as "an independent investor," "a partner in his father's conglomerate," "the heir to America's foremost iron and steel fortune," "the Narcissus of Whalenburg," and "the Golden Orphan of the Last Tycoon." Now I understood why the public relations people had guaranteed only the dissemination of the story, not the copy itself, which was phrased by the columnists to give it the appearance of social comment, though what they actually revealed in their pieces was the adulterous marriage of gossip as big business and the American press as a medium of free expression.

What I anxiously waited for finally took place: Karen telephoned me about my London escapade, saying, "I didn't know you had a penchant for easy drama—or is it easy actresses?"

I pretended not to know what she was talking about. "What drama?"

"It's all over town. I haven't been able to open a paper without running into pictures of you drooling over Louise Hunter."

I feigned nonchalance. "I like Louise, and I like to see her once in a while," I said. "She knows a lot about theater."

"She certainly knows how to get herself written about," said Karen with a tone of professional jealousy.

"She is a talented actress," I said, "and she deserves her popularity. She has worked very hard to gain it."

"I'll bet she has," said Karen. "Harder than she has at her marriage."

"What do you mean? The last time I saw them, Frank and Louise seemed quite close," I bluffed.

"The last time is right. They've split!" Karen exclaimed. "Yesterday Frank filed for divorce. He is naming you as 'the other man' in Louise's life. His lawyers must love all those pictures of you, Mr. Financier himself, hugging Mrs. Frank Hunter!"

Stunned, I asked, "Where did you hear this?"

"For one thing, it's in the papers. For another, I have friends who know them." She paused. "Louise's agent is also furious. The play's producers have told him that because of her conduct, Louise has blown any chance she had to star in the film version of the play. By the way," she added, "when you and I went to see *The Financier*, why didn't you tell me you had fucked Louise Hunter?"

"What for?" I asked. "We all have our Rawleighs. Like Gloucester in *King Lear*, 'Better I were distract: so should my thoughts be sever'd from my griefs.' Besides," I added, "though you may be everything to Rawleigh, Louise is not my whole world—just another bridge to distraction."

Karen told me with bitterness that I think she is in command of her life, but that whenever she attempts to convey to me who she is, she feels like the last surviving inhabitant of one of the Hermit Islands, the only one still speaking her tribe's language, who knows that when she dies, the tribe's language will die with her. Then, still angry about the incident with Louise Hunter, Karen turned on me. "For most of us, to become free, we would have only to cast off our responsibilities, but you, Jonathan, you are responsible to no one; your pocket money alone could buy the entire stage my life revolves on: the model agency, the photographers' studios, the fashion magazines, the cosmetics companies. You could produce a play, a movie, or a TV series, own a newspaper, or entertain the world's most exciting people. You could travel or live anywhere in the world. You could finance a new church, start a revolution, become a missionary or an anarchist. You could give in to the senses, discover new pleasures, delay aging. You could be what Ophelia imagined Hamlet to be: 'the courtier's, soldier's, scholar's eyes, tongue, sword. The glass of fashion and the mould of form, the observ'd of all observers.' Each day you live could be the equivalent of a decade in anyone else's life, Jonathan, because by speeding up experience you could in effect slow down the passage of time. Instead, you live your life as if a decade meant less to you than a single day, and you waste even that on the Louise Hunters of this world. Why?"

Karen has obviously scrutinized all the diaries I kept and the notes I wrote during my life abroad. If I ever had any doubts about whether I had made myself too accessible in them, or not accessible enough, she dispelled them by sending me as a gift a silver wall plaque with the following quote engraved on it:

Total Depravity

The free gifts, which belong to health, were taken away from man after his fall; the natural gifts, which cannot lead him to health, have been corrupted and polluted... Man's understanding is so entirely alienated from the justice of God, that he cannot imagine, conceive, or understand anything but wickedness, iniquity, and corruption. Seemingly his heart is so poisoned with sin, that he can produce only perversity.

Our nature is not only void and destitute of all good; but it is also so fertile in all types of evil, that it cannot be idle. It is that all the parts of man, from his understanding to his will, from his soul to the flesh, are soiled and entirely full of this concupiscence, or rather, to make it short, that man is nothing more than corruption.

Waiting, then, we see flesh desiring all loop-
holes through which it thinks of transferring else-
where the guilt of its vices.

—John Calvin, of Geneva

On an enclosed card, she had written, "To Jonathan,
whose roots are branches now, from Karen."

"We've never met, Mr. Whalen, but I had the good
fortune to meet your mother about two years after your
father's death. Shortly before we met, several of my articles
on the Byzantine period had been published in popular
magazines, and I was beginning to earn a reputation as an
archaeologist. Through my work I had met a Turkish an-
tique dealer who sold your mother a large collection of art
objects, among them many she had sought to acquire for
some time. In gratitude, that spring your mother invited the
dealer to stay for a week as her guest in New York. One
day he invited me to lunch, to meet Mrs. Whalen, and soon
after she invited me to dine with her. After dinner she
proudly showed me her newly acquired objects. On the
following day I sent her some of my books, having first
underlined certain passages that might interest her.

"The moment I met her, I found your mother very
attractive, Mr. Whalen. The truth is, I became enraptured
by her. You might ask, had Mrs. Whalen been an ordinary
office girl, would I have been so captivated? But you see,
she was not ordinary. She was Katherine Whalen, widow
of Horace Whalen. Just as an office girl is inseparable from
her uneventful existence, your mother was inseparable from

her past, as well as from the Byzantine splendor of her environment—her home, her wardrobe, her jewelry, her collections.

"That's how it began. From then on I saw her twice, perhaps three times a week. We went to the theater, to galleries and lectures, and we talked about everything: the miniature mosaics of Saint John Chrysostom, the icons of the Forty Martyrs of Sebaste, your mother's collections of Byzantine seals and Coptic tapestries, my writing projects, her marriage to Horace Whalen, even your mysterious whereabouts. We would meet each other only when your mother felt at her best, free to enjoy my company as much as I enjoyed hers.

"I might as well tell you, Mr. Whalen, that for a long time there was no physical intimacy between your mother and me, and regardless of whether we met at her invitation or mine, I always paid the check.

"Keep in mind that I am not a rich man, Mr. Whalen. My father was an insurance broker who left no estate. I support my mother, who lives in Florida. When I met Mrs. Whalen, I had about seventy-five thousand dollars invested in various stocks and about fifteen thousand in a savings account. In the fifteen most productive years of my life, that's all I had managed to save from the royalties of my books. I had always lived a carefully planned life, but whenever Mrs. Whalen and I went out for the evening, I spent more in one night than I normally would have spent on entertainment in a month. Finally I was forced to decide which was more important: my financial security or my enjoyment of the company of a woman unlike any I had ever known or would ever meet again. I chose your mother.

"When we became lovers, your mother insisted that we should be discreet. She didn't want to cause gossip that could hurt you or embarrass her, her friends, or your family's company. As you know, out of faithfulness to the memory of her husband, your mother did not plan to marry again. To make our relationship less apparent, whenever we visited places where she was well known, your mother would invite one of her older lady friends to go with us.

"Because of our mutual interests, we decided that we would travel together to places neither of us had ever seen. At that time your mother was not suffering from the illness that later affected her. She loved to travel, she enjoyed good food, and she was a marvelous companion.

"As your mother felt obliged to travel only first-class, she took it upon herself to pay our transportation and hotels. She would request the largest suites, one for herself and, out of discretion, another reserved in my name; the hotel management was always asked to put additional staff at her disposal, and the charge for all these people was included in the hotel bill, which was paid directly by the local branch of your family bank.

"Not that your mother didn't pay attention to her money; she was quite concerned with the stock market. Once, for instance, when we were in Venice, she heard from her brokers that the market was very bearish. During lunch on the terrace overlooking the Grand Canal, she told me that the recession had gotten worse, and that the previous day her estate had lost, on paper at least, close to sixty-two million dollars. In the afternoon she asked for the latest American newspapers, and when one of the hotel managers delivered them, she joked that, given the dismal state of America's economy, the Soviet Union's *Pravda* would probably be more accurate than *The Wall Street Journal* at predicting what would happen on the Street. Immediately the hotel manager offered to bring your mother the latest edition of *Pravda*.

"When she asked him where, in Venice, he could get *Pravda*, he replied that he had a subscription to it, and that he would be glad to translate any articles that particularly interested her. Surprised, your mother asked him how he came to subscribe to such a newspaper. He admitted to being a Communist, to having studied in the Soviet Union, even to being a secretary of the local party cell. Taken aback—for the hotel, which catered only to the finest clientele, was among her favorites—Mrs. Whalen asked the man what he thought about America. 'It has become a warmongering country, madam,' he answered. 'And one that bodes no good for the future of mankind.' 'How could you possibly say that?' said Mrs. Whalen. 'And who has given you such an idea?' The manager bowed politely. 'Among others, I learned this from a man you yourself have known quite well.' 'I can't believe that,' said your mother. 'Who was it?' 'Mr. Horace Sumner Whalen, madam. Mr. Whalen said this in the speech he delivered while visiting the Soviet Union, and its entire text was carried by *Pravda*, even though, apparently, only small fragments of it appeared in American newspapers.'

"But getting back to what I was saying, because your mother's expenses during our travels were paid by the bank, she seldom carried any cash, and whenever she needed extra money, the hotel's concierge would lend it to her, then include it on her bill. I took it upon myself to do the tipping, the only financial responsibility that I thought I could afford to assume in our travels, and when the need for gratuities arose, it was I who handed them out. Eventually, in order to be always prepared, I began to carry an attaché case filled with ones, fives, tens, and twenties for use in restaurants, nightclubs, taxis, garages, ships, trains, airports, inns, spas, clinics—wherever.

"As I recall, I gave about ten dollars to each hall porter, ten to a headwaiter, five to a wine steward, twenty-five each to ship stewards and pursers, five to a bell captain, five to each maid and valet, forty or fifty to each private museum or archaeological site guide, one hundred to a hotel manager, and twenty-five to a desk clerk in charge of theater tickets; every hired seamstress got forty, and hotel telephone operators, secretaries, chauffeurs, masseuses, beauticians, and hairdressers got twenty-five each. Naturally, knowing who your mother was and seeing how comfortably she liked to live and travel, most people who were of assistance to us—whether Swiss sleeping car attendants or Iranian mule drivers—expected to be handsomely tipped. Even though I tipped them, they believed the money came from Mrs. Whalen, and I can assure you none of them was ever disappointed. I was generous to a fault: by the end of the second year of my relationship with your mother, out of all of my savings I had only two thousand dollars left, and I was nowhere near finishing my book about the historical consequences of the baptism of Theodosius, son of Emperor Maurice, in the year 584.

"I never mentioned to your mother the dilemma that tipping had created for me. How could I? In my relationship with her, it was the only financial obligation that I had assumed, and it was the least that I, a mature and professional man, could do for her. You see, I loved Katherine more than I had ever loved anyone, and to explain that I had run out of money tipping waiters would have meant admitting a total financial dependence on her from then on, which would have brutally distorted my real need of her. If I couldn't afford it, too bad for me. But I resolved never to speak of it.

"I wrote her instead that I had to finish my book quickly and wouldn't be able to see her until it was completed. Your mother took my letter as proof of my not wanting her anymore, and within a week she was gone."

Another contribution has been made to my family's oral history. After attending a service at the Madison Avenue Presbyterian Church, once my mother's favorite, I was politely accosted by an elegantly dressed older gentleman. "Are you, sir, by chance, Jonathan Whalen, the son of the late Mrs. Katherine Whalen?" he asked in a heavily accented staccato English. When I told him I was, he introduced himself as Mr. Vladimir Borys, shoemaker and owner of a small East Side custom-made shoe manufacturing establishment. As we walked toward my hotel, he told me that for over a decade he had hand-made and occasionally repaired the shoes of my parents.

According to Mr. Borys, although my father was content with a couple of pairs of new shoes every two or three years, my mother habitually ordered a pair or two every month.

"Mrs. Whalen's feet troubled her," said Mr. Borys. "The foot surgery she underwent several times did not seem to help, and she sought relief from her pain in the well-fitting shoes I made for her." Mr. Borys reflected, then continued. "I was heartbroken when I found that transmitter in the heel of one of her shoes. You see, I thought I might have contributed, inadvertently, to her depression."

Feigning familiarity with the incident, I asked, "How did you happen to come across the transmitter?"

Mr. Borys looked anxious. "Mrs. Whalen had stopped by for a fitting for a new pair of shoes, and I noticed that the heel on one of the shoes she was wearing was slightly crooked. I offered to fix it on the spot, and as I removed the heel I discovered inside a tiny metal object—a cleverly hidden miniature transmitter. Of course I showed it to your mother, and once she realized that someone was spying on her, she became terribly upset."

"What happened next?" I asked.

"She summoned me to check all her other shoes. Most

of them contained transmitters. And since I also fixed Mrs. Whalen's handbags once in a while, I checked them as well. Like her shoes, most of them had transmitters hidden in them."

Mr. Borys and I came to my corner.

"Mrs. Whalen confided in me later," he said, as if to hand me a final gift of his memory of my mother before parting, "that an electronics expert she hired had removed other such transmitters hidden in her cars, as well as in all her telephones."

"Did she ever tell you who had installed these listening devices, or why she was kept under surveillance?" I asked.

"One day when she came to my shop, your mother seemed quite ill—almost not herself," said Mr. Borys, changing his tone. "Forgive me, but I think she might have been drinking. She told me that the surveillance still continued, and that she had found out that the orders to have her followed had come from someone high up in your father's company—a man who was also your godfather."

"Did she know why she was being followed?"

"Your mother told me that she was seeing a man she was very fond of—maybe even loved. He was a bit younger than herself, a writer of history and archaeology. Apparently your godfather suspected that this writer was after your mother's money, and that's why he put her under surveillance."

Standing in a bar in Pittsburgh, Whalen ordered a drink. Close by, two men glanced at him and continued talking. Fragments of their conversation reached him above the din of the jukebox and the television set. The bartender rinsed a glass, filled it with liquor, and pushed it toward Whalen.

Whalen leaned back and looked along the bar.

Resting her elbow on the counter, a young black girl settled herself on a stool, her legs dangling, her eyes fixed on Whalen. She was alone and on the prowl. Her looks and her manner aroused him, and he ordered another drink and moved over beside her.

"I hope you don't mind my squeezing in here," he said, putting his hand next to hers on the counter.

"I don't mind," she answered.

"I wonder if you might like to go out of town with me for a day or two."

"What for?" she asked.

He looked straight at her. "I like your looks. A girl like you could make me do things no white woman could."

She grinned. "Do you always come on as strong as that?"

"Only if I want the girl to come on strong right back."

"What else did you have in mind?"

"To see a house. It's in Whalenburg, West Virginia. A nice drive from Pittsburgh," said Whalen.

The girl listened, sipping her drink. "Why should I go for a ride to some faraway barn with someone I don't even know? What's in it for me?"

"Money—and you might also like to see the house. It's quite a place, with lots of rooms, old furniture, paintings."

She played with her glass. "Are you going to rip off something there?"

"Just my memories," said Whalen. "As a kid, I used to live in that house. It's been closed for years now, but there's still a lot of my stuff in it. I just don't feel like walking alone through all those rooms."

"Let me get this straight. Now, in the middle of the

night, you want to visit a ghost house outside of Shits-burgh?" She laughed.

Whalen smiled. "My mother used the same name for this town."

"What is it that you want me to do there?" the girl asked, eyeing him suspiciously.

"Nothing that you haven't already done, nothing that you don't know how to do," said Whalen. "And nothing that will hurt you while you do it." He paused. "I'll also make it worth your while. Do you have anything better to do?"

"No," she said, finishing her drink. "We don't have ghost houses in my family. And I always need cash. Do you know your way to Whalenburg?"

"That's all I know," said Whalen. "Let's go."

The blacks in this country make me think of certain birds I saw in Africa. Swooping up and down on air currents, they fly for hours with no effort, but on touchdown they pitch forward, skidding along on their stubby legs, straining to withstand the crash landing. Unable to slow down, they try to dig into the sand with their bellies, necks, and beaks, and when they are thus absorbed they will collide with anything in their path. Often you see one of these birds break its wing, its leg, its beak, or its spine. Unable to fly, the damaged creature will then struggle this way and that on the ground until it reaches its nest in the thicket. Watching these crippled birds, I always wondered whether they envied the freedom of their airbone relatives or whether they were glad to be grounded, with the earth for their only medium and haven, past their trial, never to soar again.

All the walls of the house, those painted with delicate designs as well as those covered with tapestries, portraits, or dim landscapes, had faded and become pastel. The carpets smelled musty, the parquet floor had long gone unwaxed. Whalen lifted the dust covers to look at the chairs; their delicate legs and intricately carved arms were still sharp in his memory. Small tables still stood in familiar places near window nooks and love seats, waiting to be used again, refusing to lose their purpose along with their polish.

In his mother's bathroom, he quickly found his way to the secret built-in medicine cabinet under the sink. A few scattered vials of drugs, some of them professional samples, littered the shelves. Recalling how easily the family doctor had given her these drugs, Whalen picked up two sample packages and read through all the instructions, indications, and contraindications: "for the relief of symptoms of depression"; "for the reversal of psychotic behavior patterns"; "for management of overt hostility assoicated with organic brain disease"; "recommended only for patients under close medical supervision"; "to alleviate severe apathy, agitation, psychomotor retardation"; "extreme caution required when given to patients with history of alcoholic consumption"; "overdosage may produce hysteria, stupor, coma, shock, respiratory depression, and death."

The girl switched off the overhead light in his mother's bedroom and turned on a smaller one in the walk-in closet. Leaving the closet door open, she eased her stockings down, unhooked her bra and hung it on the doorknob, and stepped out of her underpants. Without a word she walked over to Whalen, reached down, took his hand and raised it to her breast, then pushed it lower and pressed it against her warm, dry flesh. She threw back her head and sat down next to him on the bed, waiting.

In the dim light that came from the closet, Whalen studied her squared-off cheekbones, her slanted eyes, her full-lipped mouth and the way the sharp features of her head contrasted with the smooth contours of her body.

He thought of her as his prey, an African girl whom he, the white hunter from across the sea, might eye in Mombasa. Her life in the slums of Pittsburgh was a jungle to him, and to her he was as out of reach as his childhood in this house now was. That's why, with her, he could give in to his urges and abandon himself to what he would otherwise dare only in thoughts. By imposing his desire on the girl, he might also arrive at surrendering to her, and in his surrender he might succeed in drawing her into the scheme of his thought. Here, among the relics of his past, he might escape the past with this black girl, who on her own could never have entered this house while there was life in it.

A hunter about to be freed by his prey, he kissed her neck, slid down on the bed, and kissed her mound. She threw her thigh over his head, and poising herself astride his face, she forced herself down, her flesh grinding against his lips, enveloping him until, as he sought to give her pleasure, he was left scarcely able to breathe, fighting for air that now only she could give him. His pulse raced. Once, skin-diving in Africa, he had come upon a sea snake, the unchallenged ruler of the deep, coiled in the thick coral. In a surge of fright he had moved away, but the snake had followed effortlessly behind him until it spiraled serenely at his side, its lidless eyes watching him. He remembered how quickly he had tired, how defeated he had felt, and how he had hated that creature, which, equipped by nature with only one light lung, could breathe more effectively than he could, for all of the two big tanks he carried on his back. Now, aroused by the girl and no longer able to control himself, he envied the snake's ability to slow down, to control the pace of its heartbeat even at the peak of its excitement.

He approached the bed and stood quietly beside it. She was asleep, her head on the pillow at the level of his knees. He looked at the remnants of her makeup, cracked by tiny wrinkles under her eyes and matted with perspiration at the base of her nose. As he rested his hand on the blanket, it occurred to him that she was only pretending to be asleep, actually anticipating his touch. He drew his hand back.

Whalen opened a portfolio that contained various letters. Some of them were letters he himself had received in the past. The first one was written on his father's business stationery.

Dear Jonathan,

On July 27, I sent back to the summer camp a form indicating that you would be coming home by train, and I enclosed our check for $53.61. The camp's people will purchase your train ticket and give you $15.00 traveling money to cover meals and other incidentals. To make you comfortable, we are getting you a parlor-car seat in the Pullman. They will serve you lunch and dinner in the same car, and the porter will tell you when to get off. You can give him a dollar tip for the trip to Pittsburgh, and the same to the waiter. Your schedule is as follows: on August 18th, the camp closes at 10 A.M. The people at the camp will put you on the train at Plymouth, Indiana. Your train's name is the Fort Pitt. It leaves at 10:56 A.M. and arrives in Pittsburgh at 7:45 P.M. You can tell the porter I will be on hand to meet you. I'm sure he knows who I am. Enjoy the rest of your stay at the camp, and come back full of vim and vigor. Have a good trip.

Cordially,
Your father

He picked up another letter neatly typed on the company stationery.

My dear Son,

I have received two letters from you, and they give me much pleasure because, as you know, I miss you very much and am looking forward to being with you in another eight or nine days. Your mother and I talk about you every day. Since she is more in touch with your school than I am, she knows how well you are getting along there, which of course I expected. I'm glad that, where you are, the weather is fine because it's anything but fine here, raining and altogether disagreeable. I assume you are playing tennis and swimming every day, which is good for your health. Keep up the good work and take care of yourself. We look forward to seeing you soon.

With lots of love,
Father

On the letter's bottom-left corner were traces of a sentence that was typed, then erased, by his father's secretary: "Dictated but not read."

Another old letter, this one from the office of the mayor of Pittsburgh, was addressed to Jonathan James Whalen, Esq.

Dear Jonathan,

No words of mine can ease your sorrow at the loss of your father, but I want you to know that my thoughts are with you. There is little else we mortals can do than to remember your father in our prayers.

My warmest regards,
John Lee Overholt,
Mayor

The next letter, from the dean of his college at Yale, Jonathan recalled well; he had received it shortly before going abroad.

The committee has reviewed your record for the spring semester. As you know, you failed English, political science, history, and anthropology. You also failed to raise your Grade Point Index to the minimum requirement. As your record to date gives no substantive proof that you are capable of academic discipline and achievement, it is the committee's recommendation that you be dismissed from the college. After due consideration, I have accepted their recommendation and have instructed the registrar that you shall not be permitted to enroll for the coming semester. I regret the necessity of this action and wish you every success in the future.

In the same stack, he found a letter to his father, handwritten on White House stationery and signed by the President.

My Dearest Friend,

As I embark on this campaign of putting my pledges into effect for the benefit of our country, one of my great comforts is the knowledge that our party will not lack the needed funds to bring the message of my electoral crusade to all our fellow Americans. I cannot begin to thank you for your donation—the most generous in our party's history—but I wish to assure you of my deep gratitude; both as a friend and as a Republican, you have done a magnificent job.

With all best wishes to you, Katherine, and Jonathan—

Next to the President's letter he came across a Yale University honorary Doctor of Laws citation.

Horace Sumner Whalen, leader of an industry and founder of a city, your career has been a living example of the American dream. Combining the resources of West Virginia with those of other places, you have caused a riverside to blossom forth as a rich industrial town, which bears your name. You have contributed significantly to your country's industrial potential—a major factor in maintaining our present uneasy peace, and the foundation for an increasingly high standard of living. Sensitive to the dangerous state of world affairs, you have devoted yourself to understanding the causes of present world tensions and to alerting your countrymen to the need for intelligent action to avoid the tragedy of another world war.

In recognition of your notable achievements as industrialist, philanthropist, citizen, and student of international affairs; by virtue of the authority vested in me as president of the University, and with the approval of the Board of Governors, I confer upon you the degree of Doctor of Laws with all its rights, honors, and privileges.

Whalen picked up a folder of newspaper clippings and leafed through the two-inch headlines from New York and Pittsburgh newspapers. HORACE WHALEN DROWNS. INDUSTRY EMPIRE BUILDER, THE SEA'S VICTIM. CIVIC LEADERS MOURN WHALEN. HORACE SUMNER WHALEN DEAD.

Other clippings gave fragments of his father's biography: "During his exemplary life, Horace Sumner Whalen turned a single rolling mill into a multibillion-dollar empire that was located initially in Whalenburg, a West Virginia township Whalen founded and later named after himself. Branded by his enemies 'the lone wolf' of American business and 'the feudal lord of Whalenburg,' Whalen took on the most powerful adversaries: American presidents, Con-

142

gress, the federal bureaucracy, organized labor, and heavy industry itself." "Born of Calvinist lineage in the Mesabi mining region of Minnesota, Horace Whalen never completed his elementary education." "At the age of thirteen, Horace Whalen got his first job as an office boy with a local iron-mining company. Advancing rapidly to positions of increasing responsibility, at the age of twenty Mr. Whalen became a plant manager. Two years later he founded his own company, which has never shown a loss." "The death of Horace Sumner Whalen writes the final chapter in the saga of the rise of American heavy industry and the exemplary individualists who were its leaders. Andrew Carnegie, Henry Clay Frick, Charles Schwab, F. F. Jones, Henry Phipps, Jr., Ernest Tenet Weir, and Horace Whalen are the heroes of that story. They were tough men engaged in a tough business. And they helped to make this nation tough." "A devoted Christian fundamentalist, Horace Sumner Whalen many years ago told reporters that he started every day with the same prayer, for inspiration read Dickens, Thoreau, Walt Whitman, and Robinson Jeffers, and at least once a week listened to Bach's Toccata and Fugue in D Minor." "Whalen said once that if he was fond of the American Constitution and its plea for the distribution of power, it was not because he believed that all men equally deserved to exercise power, but because the Constitution properly bore out John Calvin's notion of man's natural corruption, as expressed in his *Institutes*: that 'the vice or imperfection of men therefore renders it safer and more tolerable for the government to be in the hands of many . . . and that if any one arrogate to himself more than is right, the many may act as censors and masters to restrain his ambition.'"

Jonathan picked up a program of the Annual Dinner of the Institute of American Heavy Industry. The dinner that year had been given in honor of his father, who was a past president of the institute. At the center of the program's cover was a raised aluminum-foil medallion engraved with the running bull, the institute's symbol, and inscribed with the words "A Great and Growing Country." In addition to the opening remarks by Horace Whalen, the evening's main attraction was a speech, "SEATO—Power for Peace," by General Thomas B. F. Gertner, U.S. Supreme Allied Commander, Southeast Asia. The menu consisted of bisque de langouste with sherry, croutons, filet de boeuf à la mode, golden fleurons, salad, frozen soufflé Alaska, cherries jubilee flambé, petits fours, and demitasse. Jonathan tried to picture his father unfolding his napkin, appreciating the meal, and applauding politely after the speeches.

The content of other newspaper articles and the transcripts of certain public speeches indicated that Horace Whalen might have been more disposed to having his son become a draft dodger than to applauding General Gertner, the evening's principal speaker. Only a few days before that dinner, Horace Whalen had been the guest on television's *Face the Nation*. Introduced as a propagandist for a strongly antimilitaristic point of view, he was questioned by the country's top journalists, and in the TV program's transcript he was quoted as saying: "Half of our every dollar and over eighty percent of our energy budget goes to our military. Even though with our current atomic resources we could blow up every big Soviet city fifty times over, we produce daily two additional nuclear bombs, each of which has a megatonnage higher than all the bombs dropped by both sides during World War II. Half of this generation's scientists and engineers have been working for the Department of Defense, experimenting with over twenty thousand designs for future weaponry—from self-guiding missiles and killer satellites to death rays and lasers capable of melting tanks, planes, and satellites. Meanwhile, the cost of only

one American attack plane represents two times the cost of
our total national budget for making our water safe for
drinking! We have become so entrenched in and accustomed
to the war economy and war production that most Americans
believe that only a new war, or military spending that leads
to one, can give us full employment and production. Yet,
as history teaches us, our war economy can only make us
a country given over to galloping inflation, not to mention
industrial and human waste in gigantic porportions."

In a separate album, mounted under transparent plastic
casings, Jonathan found clippings about his mother. "Mrs.
Katherine Furston Peck Whalen, one of America's richest
women, died last night. With grace and ease, Mrs. Whalen
bore the mantle of grande dame of American industry. She
presided over her forty-room mansion in Whalenburg, and
after her husband's death continued to maintain homes in
New York, Southampton, and Palm Springs, as well as a
favorite yacht in the Mediterranean. She also presided over
the family's formidable Byzantine art collection and founded
the Katherine Whalen Center for Byzantine Studies in Whalenburg, the township that still houses the steel mills of
Whalen Industries. Often listed among the world's ten best-
dressed women, Mrs. Whalen owned jewelry that was es-
timated to be worth millions of dollars." "With the death
of Horace Sumner Whalen, Mrs. Whalen inherited over a
quarter of a billion dollars in tax-free municipal bonds
alone." "Mrs. Whalen was reportedly grief-stricken for
years after her husband's death, despite the comfort she
derived from an only son, Jonathan." "Following her late
husband's instructions, Mrs. Whalen has left her entire estate to Jonathan James Whalen, her son." "Jonathan
Whalen, the only child of Horace and Katherine Whalen,
has been living abroad, where he combines study with
travel."

Jonathan came across a folder of press clippings labeled "Distortions" in his mother's handwriting. It contained newspaper and magazine articles that questioned the official family statement attributing the cause of his father's death to a heart attack suffered after a swim in front of the family's Rhode Island vacation home. The articles spoke of Mrs. Jean Roberts as "the other woman" in his father's life. Mrs. Roberts was a vice-president of one of his father's subsidiary companies. Some reporters noted that while Mrs. Whalen restricted herself to the houses in Whalenburg, Southampton, New York, and Palm Springs, Horace Whalen often used the Rhode Island house for business purposes. According to other reports, Mrs. Roberts owned a nearby Rhode Island house, paid for with the help of a substantial loan from one of Horace Whalen's companies.

Denying the family version of Horace Whalen's death, the articles produced their own facts: that when the ambulance arrived at the scene of the accident, Mrs. Roberts was wearing an evening gown; that Horace Whalen, clad only in swimming trunks, was found dead on the beach in front of Mrs. Roberts's house; that late October, after sunset, was an unlikely time for a swim; that Horace Whalen's clothes were found scattered about in Mrs. Roberts's bedroom; that the subsequent autopsy revealed alcohol in Horace Whalen's blood and stomach. Other papers, quoting one of the paramedics, conjectured that a substantial time must have elapsed between Whalen's attack and Mrs. Roberts's summoning of the ambulance, a time during which Mrs. Roberts had quite likely dressed herself, slipped the swimming trunks on her dying lover, and managed to walk

146

him down to the beach, where he collapsed and died. There was speculation that, had Mrs. Roberts telephoned the ambulance the minute Horace Whalen was stricken, the paramedics could have saved his life, though, perhaps, not his public image: that of the proud man who had never surrendered to idle pleasures.

At first the articles jolted Jonathan. Not that he was shocked by the presence of Mrs. Roberts in his father's life—in her photographs she appeared to be a nondescript, slightly plump woman; what shocked him was her age. Mrs. Roberts was fifteen years older than Katherine Whalen.

Jonathan's thoughts were then flooded by the image of his father's death. He could see him making love to Mrs. Roberts. Suddenly his father choked, struggling for breath, clutching his chest, and sweating and trembling he rose above her, only to collapse on top of her. Mrs. Roberts screamed; then in panic she eased out from under his weight; then, turning him faceup, she began pouring champagne over his head and splashing his chest with ice water and begging him not to die. Blurting words, coughing and whispering, his father pointed to the beach. Mrs. Roberts understood. She forced a pair of his swimming trunks onto him, then helped him to stand up, but his father, unable to carry his own weight, fell to the floor. Mrs. Roberts helped him onto the bed, pleading with him to rest while she put on clothes because she must not be found naked. Then she helped him get up, and with his arm over her shoulder she dragged him across the bedroom, the living room, the glass-enclosed veranda, across the terrace, down the wooden staircase, along the narrow path between the grassy dunes, and onto the beach, his father wheezing, heaving, gasping for air all the while, leaning on Mrs. Roberts for support, his feet plowing the sand. They were now at the ocean, with its mist on their faces, their ankles in waves. There his father stumbled for the last time and fell. Jonathan saw the foam spill over him.

Another folder contained several sheets of unused American postage stamps bearing his father's portrait. A letter signed by the postmaster general was attached to one of the sheets.

Dear Mrs. Whalen:

We are happy to present you with the first official sheet of this new stamp commemorating your husband's pioneering role in American industry. Additional sheets will be available for members of your family, the directors and officers of your company, and others whom you designate.

Jonathan could not remember his mother's telling him about this commemorative issue. Nor could he remember ever receiving a letter from her postmarked with the Whalen stamp. He wondered whether she had been displeased that the nation's tribute to Horace Sumner Whalen should have been paid on a stamp with such a low denomination. Now, after years of two-digit inflation rates, not even a postcard could be mailed with one of them.

The memories triggered no emotion. Jonathan recalled coming home from summer camp. A company limousine was waiting for him at the Pittsburgh station. He sat next to the chauffeur and read the passing signs—Sweetheart Brands, Forge and Pipe Works, Half-Moon Island, Moon Run Road, Moontour Run—thinking how strange the familiar names sounded. He could hear the chauffeur reverently telling him that the Peter Tarr blast furnace had produced cannonballs used by Oliver Hazard Perry in the War of 1812; that his father, Horace Sumner Whalen, was sole owner of all the land surrounding the furnace for miles; and that one day he, Jonathan Whalen, would own all that land.

In another drawer he found a yearbook from the H. L. Mencken College for Girls, and he turned the pages until he came to his mother's picture. She looked girlish and frail and had unusually long hair.

A short paragraph next to the picture noted that Katherine Furston Peck was an honor student, had won first prize in the Alpha Omega poetry contest, and was a member of Cum Laude, the student council, and the yearbook staff. She was voted most likely to succeed, wittiest, and most attractive. She participated in a number of sports, and she was president of the Byzantine Antiquity Club, vice-president of the Debating Club, honorary chairman of Parents' Weekend, and a Foreign Travel Society representative.

Printed in italics were her girl friends' fond tributes to her: "Kitty's terrific sense of humor makes her one of the most popular girls in her class. No wonder the boys flock all the way from Pittsburgh to find out what goes on behind that flashing smile!" "She's impeccably groomed and marvelous at backgammon, and we'll long remember singing to her expert guitar accompaniment." "Her horseback riding and tennis game are great, and she's a natural at French and German." "Her family's convertible has been the vehicle for numerous fun-filled outings."

Tucked inside the yearbook, Jonathan found an essay by Katherine Peck. "Searching for a stage on which to enact the drama of free men engaged in free enterprise," she wrote, "American industry has evolved an architecture unique in the history of mankind: the skyscrapers, those magnificent towers of steel and glass, are the very soul of *Homo Americanus*. Yet once man has erected such noble structures, he still perseveres, never satisfied, never stopping to enjoy the fruits of his labors. These colossal creations are America's greatest contribution to art, and the steel industry is our nation's monument to America's restless energy."

Jonathan flipped through the yearbook. In the back pages he came across an advertisement with a youthful photograph of his father at the top of it. "Dollars—dollars—dollars: As graduates you need funds. Save as regularly as you eat, or you will become financially undernourished. Don't wait any longer. Open a checking and savings account now at one of the many branches of the Whalen Bank of Commerce and Savings." He wondered if young Katherine Peck had pondered this photograph of Horace Whalen before she met him; perhaps it was this picture in her yearbook, in fact, that first prompted her to seek employment in the Whalen company's steel and glass skyscraper in Pittsburgh.

Jonathan picked up a leather-bound volume of *David Copperfield* and opened it to a page with a bent corner. Someone, perhaps his father, had underlined a short passage in which the sight of Steerforth's house starts David on "a long train of meditations . . . mingled with childish recollections and later fancies, the ghosts of half-formed hopes, the broken shadows of disappointments dimly seen and understood, the blending of experience and imagination."

He reached for a volume of poems by Robinson Jeffers and opened it to a page indicated by a bookmark. In a poem called "Shine, Perishing Republic," the following was underlined:

> But for my children, I would have them keep their
>   distance from the thickening center; corruption
> Never has been compulsory, when the cities lie at
>   the monster's feet there are left the mountains.

On a page with a bent corner, in the poem "Dear Judas," someone had underlined what Lazarus says to Mary about Jesus:

> Your son has done what men are not able to do;
>   He has chosen and made his own fate.

On the bottom of the page, Horace Whalen had scribbled: "Robinson Jeffers also wrote 'To His Father,' a sonnet with this beginning:

> Christ was your lord and captain all your life,
> He fails the world but you he did not fail,

He led you through all forms of grief and strife
Intact, a man full-armed . . .

Jeffers' father, a Calvinist, was a professor of Old Testament literature at the Western (Presbyterian) Theological Seminary in Pittsburgh."

Whalen heard footsteps on the stairs, and as he turned toward the door a tall trooper entered it with his gun drawn. Whalen jumped to his feet.

"Don't you move, buddy. Get your hands up," said the trooper, motioning with the gun. Whalen raised his arms. "I found the other half, Sheriff," shouted the trooper to someone outside the door.

"Coming!" a man answered.

"Don't try anything stupid," said the trooper, his gun trained on Whalen.

"I'm not about to," said Whalen.

A stocky sheriff brought the black girl into the room. Her hands were handcuffed behind her and she looked as if she had been roughed up. When she saw Whalen with his hands raised, she managed a smile.

"Search him," said the sheriff, and as the trooper replaced his gun in his holster and moved toward Whalen, Whalen lowered his hands.

"I told you not to move, you fucker," yelled the trooper, stepping forward and slamming his fist into Whalen's face. Stunned by the blow, Whalen staggered. Jamming his knee into Whalen's back, the trooper pushed him against the wall, then quickly handcuffed him. He pulled out his pants pockets, searching for drugs.

"Outside," commanded the sheriff, waving his gun toward the door.

The four of them walked slowly down the stairs. At the front door the trooper turned off the lights. Outside the sheriff pointed at Whalen's car.

"Is this a stolen vehicle?" he asked.

"I rented it," Whalen replied.

"Rented or stolen, you left the key in the ignition. That's against the law," said the sheriff.

"My car is in a private driveway. That's not against the law."

"Listen, smart ass, don't talk back to me," snapped the sheriff. "I'll drive these two back to the station," he said to the trooper. "You follow in the stolen vehicle."

The sheriff ordered Whalen and the girl to get into the rear seat of his car and picked up the receiver of a buzzing shortwave radio. "I'm heading back with the robbery suspects. Two of them. Male Caucasian, female Negro." Then he started the car and drove down the long driveway.

"Are we under arrest?" asked Whalen.

"What do you think?" said the sheriff.

"But what for?"

"This is still Sunday, and since we don't book on Sundays, you'll have to wait until tomorrow to find out. Till then, you and your girl friend will be guests in our newly renovated jail."

They passed through the center of Whalenburg. The streets were empty, the restaurants and bars were all closed. Whalen recalled driving along these streets with his father. "A proud town for proud people," his father had said, pointing to the rows of new two-story houses built for the company's workers.

In front of the police station the trooper pulled up behind them in Whalen's car. Inside the station the trooper removed their handcuffs. "Can I talk to you alone for a moment?" Whalen asked the sheriff.

"I'm not a confessor. Talk to me here," said the sheriff. The trooper and the three policemen in the station chuckled.

"You might need to know what I have to say," Whalen said quietly.

"All right," the sheriff agreed, "but no tricks, understand?"

They went to a small side room. "Now, what is it?" asked the sheriff impatiently.

"We're in Whalenburg, isn't that right?"

"We sure are."

"Did you look at the name on my driver's license? I'm Jonathan Whalen."

The sheriff froze. Then he said, "A lot of Whalens in this country."

"But only one in Whalenburg. My father, Horace Sumner Whalen, founded this town. Now I own a lot of it."

The sheriff reached in his shirt pocket for a cigarette. "You're *our* Whalen?" he asked uneasily. "How do I know you're not lying?"

"My family's portrait is hanging on the front wall in the main lobby of the Town Hall. I am Jonathan, the boy between Katherine and Horace Whalen. I'm older now, but I haven't changed that much."

The sheriff extinguished his cigarette. No longer uncertain, he stared nervously at Whalen. "If you're Whalen's son, why didn't you tell me?"

"You didn't give me a chance," said Whalen. "Only this." He pointed at his swollen jaw.

The sheriff paced the room.

"I'll telephone the mayor from here," said Whalen. "I want to tell him I'm back—and how I was welcomed."

The sheriff stopped in front of him. "I know you're upset, Mr. Whalen," he said. "And you have good reason to be. Look, I'm really sorry all this happened. I'd be glad to—apologize."

"Apologize? I'm not offended; I'm in pain," said Whalen, touching his chin.

"We'll take you to the company's hospital."

"No need for that. But you can do something else."

The sheriff livened up. "Anything, Mr. Whalen. I sure want to make up for the inconvenience."

"Good. I want to give back to your deputy what he gave to me. I want you to hit him just as hard as he hit me."

"If I do that," said the sheriff, squirming, "he'll sue me."

"But if you won't do it, I will sue you. Let me call the mayor first," he said.

Without a word the sheriff led him back to the main room. "Hey Bob, would you come over here for a minute, please?" he said, looking sheepishly at the floor.

The trooper walked over and stood before him. The sheriff hesitated, then swung his right fist at the trooper's face. The trooper staggered back, and blood ran over his lower lip. The desk officer rushed over to steady him. The other policemen were stunned.

The sheriff rubbed his fist. "That's it. No more trouble!" He nodded pleasantly to the girl, then turned to Whalen. "You and your friend are free to leave now, Mr. Whalen. Sorry for the mess!"

Today I received a long letter from Walter Howmet. As my godfather, he clearly expects that I should seek in him a father substitute. I decided that his advice to me was given to further the interests of the company rather than my own, so instead of writing or calling him personally, I summoned Miss Berger, his executive secretary, who had taken down his letter to me, and asked her to make notes of what I was about to say.

Miss Berger, a gray-haired, well-dressed, soft-spoken spinster, felt out of place in my hotel suite and so ill at ease in my presence that when she was not looking at her notes, she could hardly look me in the eye.

"In his letter Mr. Howmet volunteers several suggestions," I said. "He thinks I should find a more permanent residence than a hotel suite, perhaps a town house large enough to entertain in, or, in case I should marry, a country estate large enough to start a family in. He suggests I sell the various houses I have inherited, but in order to strengthen my ties with the company, he advises me to keep the house in Whalenburg. He also advises me to dispose of my mother's yacht and the villas in Italy, Switzerland, and France. He assumes that I might like to spend some time in the company offices, either in Pittsburgh or New York, getting acquainted, as he put it, with the company's inner workings, or that I might wish once again to enroll at Yale."

"Yes, Mr. Whalen, I am familiar with those recommendations," said Miss Berger.

"Fine. Now I want you to let Mr. Howmet know my wishes. First, I don't intend to work for the company. No one could possibly make sense of the whole operation, so no matter where I began I could probably never master anything beyond the most immediate concerns of one department. Furthermore, Mr. Howmet either doesn't know or doesn't remember that, as a result of my failure to fulfill Yale's scholastic requirements, I was asked to leave."

"I think Mr. Howmet assumed that you would want to make up for past errors in judgment," said Miss Berger.

"I'm too old to want to make up for what others consider my failures. Another thing: had the trustees in charge of my estate, including Mr. Howmet, been truly concerned about my financial situation, they would have long ago sold all those houses and villas and collections and boats and God knows what other useless, unoccupied, highly taxed properties I've inherited from my parents. I intend to sell them now, immediately, even if it means a financial loss, and live in Manhattan, on the East River, in a small town house with windows and terrace facing the river and the United Nations. However, until the house is vacated by its present occupants, renovated, and furnished, I will remain in my suite in this hotel. And one more thing: you may also tell Mr. Howmet that from the house I will have direct access to my boat."

"Your boat, Mr. Whalen?" Miss Berger asked.

"Yes. I have bought a small boat. It sleeps two."

"Is there a marina in front of your town house?"

"No, but the building is right near the embankment, so I could easily get down to the boat by means of a ladder."

"Isn't it against the law to pick up or discharge passengers at an unauthorized place on the East River?"

"Too bad if it is. I'll have to break the law, then. The boat will be kept at the midtown marina, and each time I want it the captain will deliver it to the embankment in front of my building."

"May I ask why you need such immediate access to a boat?"

"Why shouldn't I have it? Manhattan is surrounded by rivers and by some of the most beautiful ocean beaches in the world," I said. "I also like to take long car trips, so I have obtained a car and an underground garage. Mr. Howmet buys only American goods; he will be pleased to know I've bought a Ford."

"Mr. Howmet was also concerned about servants."

"Maids, a cook, a guard, and two—maybe three— other people will live in the house with me."

Miss Berger checked her notes. "Mr. Howmet was delighted by your show of good business sense in acquiring Executive Heliways," she said, forcing a smile. "You must know that the price of that company's stock has gone up by thirty percent since you purchased it."

"I bought Executive Heliways for sentimental reasons, Miss Berger. They were the first people I did business with when I got back to America. And also because I like to fly in helicopters."

Sometimes, when I know Karen is with Susan, I feel that I am disposable, but today I took them both to dinner and now, a few hours later, I am absolutely calm, even though the meal itself was unrelentingly depressing. Susan and Karen talked for an hour while I ate and said nothing. Nevertheless, I feel as if I have finally faced something I've been avoiding for weeks.

They talked about sex as if they had never discussed it before. Susan said she finds that very few people are sexually aware. Even if they are on the make and looking for signals, she said, even if they listen to what you say, talk to you, and carefully articulate their thoughts, more often than not they are too selfish to notice how and where you glance as they talk or listen. They don't observe your posture and expression or the movements of your lips or hands, all of which indicate how you are responding to them sexually.

For my benefit Susan launched into a lecture about Karen. She said that Karen's sexuality is much stronger than her own and that Karen instantly picks up sexual feedback. Most people create sexual fantasies about others only when those individuals are not directly available, whereas whenever Karen meets a man, a woman, or a couple, she spontaneously pictures herself in bed with them. Susan speculated that men and women are drawn to Karen by her elusiveness, which makes them ever so curious about the unbridled sexuality they sense behind her cool exterior.

"Karen would make an ideal lesbian," said Susan, "because she has always been merely intrigued by men's sexuality, never attracted to it. Also, in worshiping herself as a perfect woman, she has become, in the process, fascinated by femininity—by what makes a woman perfect. Though she may be willing to accept love from a man, Karen is probably able to return love only to a woman."

Throughout the lecture Karen behaved as if she weren't with us—or as if, in Susan, she had found an echo for her own ideas.

As an afterthought, Susan remarked that she finds many of Karen's involvements incomprehensible; they are all truncated, lacking in either spiritual or sexual energy. It is sad, she went on, that Karen has never found a lover as complicated and adventurous as herself, a man or a woman through whom she could finally discover herself.

Susan finds Karen's unpredictable eroticism synonymous with being adventurous; she sees it as an indication of complexity, of sexual obsession. The truth is, Karen is merely impulsive.

I envy Karen's temperament, even though I'm frightened by it. She is never indifferent, she is seldom withdrawn, and she is always ready to change her mood. I've witnessed so many of her explosions, and her subsequent remorse, that when she swears they won't happen again, I can't believe her. She is critical of my restraint, claiming that I've been emotionally programmed by the patterns demanded by my addiction and my withdrawal, and she says it with a straight face, unable to realize how much in her own life she relies on self-imposed arbitrary patterns. Isn't she aware that unless she is well tanned she feels insecure? That while having sex, with me and apparently with others, in order to speed up her excitement and potentiate her orgasms, she more and more often depends on inhaling Onsense, the illegally manufactured and dangerous derivative of amyl, alkyl, and butyl nitrate, which, mindless of her lover, and right in the middle of her lovemaking, she will greedily breathe in straight from an ampule she breaks under her nose? That by her own admission, in search of easy sexual diversion, more and more often she joins casually met twosomes and threesomes? That at social gatherings she can no longer do without several vodkas on the rocks, which slur her speech? And what about her chain smoking? Sex with me is probably the last domain where patterns don't yet rule: after all the days and nights we have spent together talking, making love, staring at each other, and falling asleep in each other's arms, I still don't know what triggers her need of me. In every other woman I've made love to, sexuality has been a channel to her mystery, but Karen's sexuality shields her from me.

The last time I saw her she was recovering from a virus and the side effects of antibiotics. She prowled naked around her apartment, watering her already sodden plants, smoking one cigarette after another, washing a dish or spoon as soon as she used it, and from time to time glancing at me. She had just discovered, she said, that the dry cleaner had lost the sash to her new Oscar de la Renta gown. Then she said, "I've been without sex for so long now that I can't wait to start playing around again!"

I felt a cold intake of breath. Was I to be a partner in her "playing around"? Or did she merely feel that I deserved to know of her playing around with others, since for her to have sex with others was indeed to play around—around me. Reminded of her need of other lovers, I felt defeated, as if I knew in advance that each one of them would take her away from me on a path I didn't know. Later Karen took a bath, but I, immobilized by her calm and unable to master her mood, remained dressed, staring at her lean form in the foam. Each time she closed her eyes I assumed she was far away, already getting laid in her mind by her new lover.

I've been in bed for three days, unable to move, to read, or to think. The high fever is gone now, but my eyes are still tired and my body aches. The hotel waiters and maids silently come and go, feeding me, cleaning the place, doing all those chores that are usually performed for the sick person by family members or trusted servants.

I've had these symptoms before: once when I was about to leave the country and once in Rangoon after my mother's detectives found me. In those days I used to panic at the approach of the symptoms, but now I refuse to give in to them. Wednesday was the worst day. My doctor sent two nurses from Doctors Hospital to look after me, but what I needed—tender care and human concern—they couldn't give; they just sat all day in the living room giggling, watching TV, listening to music. Meanwhile, alone in the bedroom, I fought off my fear of sudden death. My heart raced and I could barely feel my pulse. Then my blood pressure seemed to drop and it was difficult for me to breathe. Still, even then, part of me refused to become engaged, so in part, at least, I was able to remain fascinated by my own terror. Then, a moment later, I was calm and no longer even felt the need for a doctor.

I thought about the black girl who had gone with me to Whalenburg. Once she found out who I was, she refused to have anything more to do with me. I had enjoyed the intensity of our lovemaking—the search for the source of sensation, the simple breakdown of the barriers the mind and body erect so easily—and I wanted to keep her with me. I even pleaded with her, promised to take her abroad, insinuated that I would make her rich. She wouldn't listen. She had made up her mind. I meant trouble to her, she said, for no matter how much I wanted her, I would soon have had enough of the sex and then I would say to her, "Go home, blackbird, there's no longer a place for you in my white cage." Fear of being used and rejected by a white man was still stronger in her than the desire for any new experience I might give her—regardless of its cost.

I wanted to call Karen but I felt drained. What's more, I knew she had better things to do than attend to a sick man.

I'll never forget the day I found her with her face caked in a natural mud mask and her body wrapped in towels that had been soaked in her own urine. As most dermatologists and beauticians know, she told me, urine is the ideal moisturizer, the best remedy for dry, cracked skin, and it has been used by beauty-conscious men and women since Babylonian times. The best of the commercially produced moisturizers all contain some urea, but Karen assured me that the natural fluid is more effective. She should know. She said she's been using it for years and that, in spite of all her sunbathing and sitting under studio lights, her skin is as smooth and lustrous as it was when she was a little girl.

Sometimes, when I was a child, I wouldn't see my father for months, and I would nourish a fantasy of him visiting hundreds of Whalenburg workers one after another and having supper in their homes. I told myself that I was lucky to have a father who was important enough to bring employment, money, and happiness to so many people and to so many other children, even though it meant that he never had enough time for me. I never imagined that my father didn't really care about me deep down; I simply knew that I was just one child, but that he had to feel responsible for the fate of every smoking chimney in Whalenburg.

If he were alive today, my father would have no idea of who I am. I doubt if he could answer the simplest questionnaire about my height, weight, or childhood illnesses. He certainly would know nothing about my tastes, my friends, or the state of my mind. And what would he, a man who refused even to travel unless it was for business, have to say about the idle years I spent abroad?

In Nepal I lived among many Tibetan refugees. To a Tibetan, death is a transition either into an incarnate state—a bodily form possessed in the past or an entirely new one—or into a discarnate state—a bodiless, immaterial form of existence. How a person has lived his life determines whether or not he will be reincarnated. Only a lama, a master of the topography of discarnation and incarnation, can perform the rituals liberating the spirit from the cycle of death and rebirth; and only he has foreknowledge of what death is like.

The rituals to be performed when death approaches are codified in the *Tibetan Book of the Dead*. If one follows these guidelines with great care, after death he will still be able to hear the voice of the lama and to act on his precepts.

As I listened to my Tibetan friends, I had an uneasy sensation that once before, as if in a previous life, I had heard the voice of the lama. Before going abroad I was shown my living trust, an agreement between my father and the trustees that placed a large part of my father's estate in an irrevocable trust for me. It instructed the trustees on how to administer the principal and interest from my father's estate during his lifetime until I came of age, and it also prescribed how the trust was to be continued in the—then so unlikely—event of his death. Unlike my father's last will, which he could change from time to time, the living trust was a final, absolute commitment of his wealth, and because of the substantial estate tax benefits and savings it involved, once it was created the law required its creator to surrender all supervisory powers to a group of trustees.

Thus, during his short lifetime, which spanned great economic and social changes, Horace Sumner Whalen, a Protestant lama from Whalenburg, created the living trust, his own *Book of the Dead*, to aid me, his uninitiated son, in the course of my future life.

"In addition to the steel, glass, aluminum, oil, and tooling industries that he and his company owned, your father was an acute land and real estate investor, Mr. Whalen.

"Shortly before his untimely death, your father realized the risks involved in owning real estate in slums, where so many blacks, Latins, Jews, and various Slavs live. Month after month many of them either refused or were unable to pay the rent, and their slums soon became an economic burden on your father's company. Now, according to law, the city must take title to any property that falls four years behind on its taxes. That's why, after a few years of ownership, acting on the excellent advice of Walter Howmet, your father relinquished some of those slum buildings; that is, he let the city take them over, at a substantial, but tax-deductible, loss to the company, which, however, in view of the company's skyrocketing profits, turned out to be a good tax shelter. Then the city had to get rid of those unprofitable buildings. It tried to unload them at public auction but there were few buyers; most of the properties remained unsold. As a result, the city was forced to offer your father's company a sizable fee to manage these slums and maintain them for their tenants—who are, incidentally, paying their rent with money received from the city's welfare rolls. Now that is a perfect dialectical example of turning public funds into private profit!

"Your father even found ways to avoid responsibility for downright abominable slum buildings the company owned in the Bowery. For instance, he would award the operating leases to other syndicates or conglomerates, which in turn would lease them to individual landlords, who, unfortunately, are often not too scrupulous. Be that as it may, your father did not personally supervise the buildings. And it was very unfair when at times the so-called liberal press referred to him as another 'invisible slumlord.' He was hardly that. And you, as your father's heir, are no more responsible for the slums than your father was."

Whalen put down the roof of his convertible and rolled down the windows. A sharp wind was blowing, and he felt small droplets of mist on his face and hands and neck. Like a huge sand yacht without its sail, the car rocked to the right and left in time with the swaying birches that arched high above the road. In front of him, the highway and the alley of trees seemed to disappear into the distance. Whalen stopped the car. He got out, wrapped his coat tighter around him, and walked toward the dense woods.

High above him the wind continued to snap the treetops back and forth, but within the shelter of the woods the ground was dry and sandy; nearby, in the tall grass, a grasshopper chirped. The sound, a voice of the earth, warmed him, and for a moment he felt at peace.

"I remember you, Mr. Whalen, when you were still a tiny kid, riding with your father in that black company limo that would stop in here to fill up. Down here in steel country, you might say folks are as patriotic as your father was; they just don't like foreign things. It's good you've gotten yourself a nice American-made automobile, Mr. Whalen. Things are rough here for anybody coming in with one of those little Japanese or German imports; the gas station attendant might just slip a couple of sugar cubes into their gas tank, courtesy of Detroit, you might say. Soon after they swallow that sugar, those little foreigners get awfully sick; they cough, spit, puff. And nobody can repair them anymore! No, sir!

"What I'm saying, Mr. Whalen, is that since Detroit don't make convertibles anymore, you were smart to have one of their Fords decapitated, like, to your own specifications. And smarter yet to hide a twelve-cylinder super-charged Ferrari gas-guzzler under that fine-looking American hood. Yes, sir! Your father would have been mighty proud of his boy!"

I went with Karen to the American Cancer Society charity ball. As we watched the gala parade of the latest whims in fashion, extravagances whipped up by the country's best designers and shown by one stunning model after another, Karen introduced me to a good-looking middle-aged man. He was an old acquaintance of hers, she said; together they had smoked and snorted the best coke in town. The man told me he was in "special investments" and said that he had learned a lot about me from Karen. At first, as if letting me in on a well-kept secret, he spoke of the advantages of smoking—rather than sniffing—cocaine in its most potent form: a free base. Since Pizarro's time, this has been a favorite pleasure of Latin American Indians. The free base is considerably more expensive than regular coke because a certain salt has been separated out of it which in regular coke represents at least one-fifth of the weight. Thanks to the proximity of the heart to the lungs, the free base, because it is smoked, is absorbed into the bloodstream quickly, and the exhilaration it causes lasts for several hours and is many times more intense than the one caused by snorting regular coke.

Just as he started to tell me how to increase the potency of the free base by smoking it in special ways, I interrupted him. I said there was hardly anything about cocaine that I did not know from past experience. I told him my doctors in Rangoon had scrupulously obtained only the best cocaine—as long as I was paying for it—for my treatment, because it is still the most effective opium disintoxicant known to science. I also said I had read most of the available literature on opium and coke, beginning with Freud, who suffered for years from depression, apathy, and anxiety and referred to cocaine as his ideal and beloved drug. Freud's enemies claimed that by overpraising the efficacy of the drug in this way in his writings, he had made it, after alcohol and opium, the third scourge of mankind.

Finally, I said that I had no longer any interest in taking drugs, and at that the man changed the subject. He began to talk about his special investments: drug dealing on a grand scale in the underdeveloped nations, to which cultivating poppies and refining opium into morphine and heroin are what producing oil is to Arab nations. Next to oil, he said, illicit drugs are the largest international moneymaker; their American sales alone generate three times as much money as the entire steel industry. Given its magnitude, the illicit drug business is an amazingly centralized, reliable, and well-run enterprise; it controls the production, supply, quality, and price of narcotics as efficiently as legitimate business controls any other international commodity. A dozen large banks act as clearing houses and laundering channels for the dope business. The man said that his contacts covered the major opium-producing countries of the "Golden Square"—Burma, Laos, Thailand, and Red China, which was the major grower and transporter. With the ease and enthusiasm of a businessman discussing iron ore or textiles or electronics, this man told me that a fifteen-hundred-pound load of pure uncut heroin, half the weight of an American sedan, costs him about eight million dollars through his contacts. A few weeks after purchase, courtesy of bribed diplomats, local officials, and air force and navy base commanders, the stuff reaches his distribution agents in New York, Miami, or Los Angeles, where its value is over three hundred million. The man pointed out that ours are inflationary times; it takes an investment of many millions of dollars to produce one Hollywood movie—and nobody can even guarantee its success. Eight million dollars is also a lot of money to invest in a once-a-year operation, but at least its profits are guaranteed—and what profits! They should not be brushed aside, even by someone of my wealth, the man said with a note of invitation in his voice. As he spoke, I could tell that he was proud of his lucrative business. In the grain of the classical American entrepreneur, he was the true descendant of those eighteenth-century merchants of New England who encouraged poppy planting in China in order to profit from the trade in "black rice," as opium was then called. Indeed, Americans were so aggressive in this venture that they were accused by both the British and the French of being unwise and indiscriminate in their opium dealings, thereby causing widespread addiction in China.

Today, the man said, he felt sorry for the "ordinarily decent" American businessmen who have to work their tails off to make the small profit that is left to them after excessive taxation. He said he makes more money in terms of actual dollars, in his pursuit of easy happiness—putting big deals together while attending parties, courting beautiful women, and traveling all over the world—than my father did in a lifetime of joyless Protestant endeavor. "You may have noticed in today's paper that the police are very proud of themselves for discovering an abandoned car with two hundred and fifty pounds of heroin in the trunk. They claimed the street value of the stuff was close to forty million dollars. Of course, the police usually exaggerate. Let's be conservative and say it was worth only fifteen million. Think of it! A suitcase in the trunk of a Ford worth fifteen million dollars! To make that kind of money, Mr. Whalen, your father needed to own mines and factories, railroads and highways, and entire company towns; he had to employ hundreds of thousands of workers; he had to talk to the unions, brown-nose politicians, be nice to the people in power. All I need, you might say, is the short-term friendship and cooperation of a few foreign diplomats, a U.S. flight sergeant, some Coast Guard customs men, and one or two smart, well-placed narcotics detectives.

"But I can see that you think all this is a dirty and vicious business, Mr. Whalen," he said. "Let me remind you that you are also engaged in corrupt enterprise, however indirectly. Do you know that the fish caught near the out-wash of some of the Whalen factories are unfit to eat because the rivers and lakes have been contaminated by nickel? That the same nickel has also damaged the livers of the workers in the Whalen company's smelters, mines, and plating factories? That as a result of the poisoning, these men and women often die young of high blood pressure, hardening of the arteries, and arthritis? It's true. So how about throwing all the humanity crap to the diseased fish too and talking business for a minute?

"When the government admits that last year Americans spent more on narcotics than they did on imported oil, I don't feel responsible for the hundreds of thousands, millions maybe, of hashish suckers, pipe masticators, and disco freaks who use spoons, tinfoil, and needles to hit themselves with the dope. You were once an addict yourself, Mr. Whalen; you know I don't make them do it. The man in the black overcoat who gives American kiddies free samples so they'll become hooked on hash is a shitty Madison Avenue myth. He has never existed and never will. Why should he give away free samples when he can sell every bag he gets?"

THE DEVIL TREE

As Whalen waited on the street corner for the light to change, a plump man with a neatly folded newspaper under his arm absentmindedly tapped the pavement with his black umbrella. Next to him, a woman wearing a cloth coat and ankle socks set down her shopping bags and rummaged through her handbag until she found a scarf and an accordion-pleated plastic rainhat.

The traffic light turned green. All three of them crossed the street, went single file into the subway, bought their tokens, and pushed through the turnstiles. Whalen stayed close to the woman. Ambling toward the front of the platform, she put a coin into a gum machine, but no gum came out. She inserted another coin. Still no gum. The woman then noticed the mirror at the top of the machine and stood on tiptoe in order to see her whole face in it. She smiled at herself, pushed some stray wisps of hair into place, then walked to a bench against the wall, sat down, arranged her bags, and rubbed her eyes. The subway rumbled as it approached. People on the platform fidgeted, shifting their weight. The train caused a draft of air and came to a stop. Whalen entered the closest car and hurried to a seat. The plump man with the newspaper was behind him getting in. As the train jolted forward, Whalen settled back and looked around. The other passengers seemed preoccupied with small details; they buttoned or unbuttoned their coats, smoothed their hair, looked at their watches, gathered their packages together, pressed umbrellas to their sides. The manner, dress, and look of every one of them betrayed an overwhelming sense of busyness, of immediate purpose. Except for the fact that he was on this subway with them, Whalen realized with a pang, he had nothing in common with these people. His stomach felt hollow and cold, his heart was in a vise. Holding his breath and bracing himself against the train's rocking, he impatiently counted the stops and promised himself never to ride the subway again.

Whalen hurried through the lobby of his hotel, his clothes dripping water onto the carpet and the floor of the elevator. Once in his suite, he changed into dry clothes, but he was still shivering with cold. He gulped down a glass of cognac, and then, having nothing better to do, he decided to go downstairs. Maybe he could sense what Karen had once called "the throbbing of the hotel lobby."

It was late. The only people in the lobby were a man at the cashier's window, an elderly woman talking on the house phone, and a plump man reading a newspaper. Whalen was about to go to the bar when he recalled that he'd seen the same plump man on the street corner and again on the subway. As Whalen glanced at him again, the man raised the newspaper in front of his face.

Whalen decided to find out whether he was being followed. He strolled casually out of the lobby. The doorman promptly called him a taxi, and when it arrived he got inside, turning to look back as the cab left the curb. Two sedans parked near the hotel immediately pulled out behind the taxi. Whalen asked the driver to go around the block. When the taxi turned the corner, the two cars followed. Whalen told the driver to take the first right turn and then the next left. The sedans were still behind him. When he asked the driver to go around the block again, the man became suspicious. Whalen explained that he had bet some friends of his that he could lose them in city traffic. He told the driver to drop him in the middle of Times Square, and as the taxi halted Whalen paid the driver and jumped out. He ducked behind a newsstand. It was still raining. Both sedans pulled to the curb, and two men got out of each and scattered in the crowd. As one of them passed near the newsstand, Whalen heard the static of a walkie-talkie. For a while Whalen mingled with the crowd, but soon he was drenched and moved into a crowded cafeteria.

Sitting at a table away from the window, his back to the street, he wondered who was paying to have him so elaborately tailed: the plump man, two cars, four men with walkie-talkies. Was it police? In spite of his previous drug history, they must surely know he was no longer buying or concealing drugs. The drug people? What for? He owed them nothing. Mafia? He remembered reading newspaper stories about people who kidnapped the rich, but he dismissed the thought. The crime syndicate worked subtly and efficiently; if they wanted him, they would have kidnapped him ten times over by now. Then who were his followers?

The coffee was weak; he felt sluggish. He thought of calling Karen but decided against it. Lately, when they talked, Karen seemed distant, probably because there was another man in her life, who was perhaps in bed with her right now. It was bad enough to be trapped in Times Square by the rain and anonymous pursuers without being reminded that he was also trapped by Karen.

Karen claims that when I seem sexually guarded, even though she's turned on by my resistance, she responds by being cold—despite the risk of scaring me off. This makes her feel Victorian, passive, alive to nothing, just there to accept sex whenever I want to give it.

I told her that even in sex I was always trying to conceal both portions of my personality: the manipulative, malevolent adult who deceives and destroys and the child who craves acceptance and love. Now I know that I have really tried to conceal the child at the expense of the adult. While my dominant concern all my life has been with not admitting needs, not asking for things, not squandering money, my worst terror has always been that I might seem helpless, and that in appearing helpless or childish I might again be judged in relation to my parents. That's why, even in my lovemaking, I manage to stay self-contained, allowing myself no extremes of pleasure or happiness. Recently Karen remarked that I must have lost my passions somewhere abroad. I wonder if she thinks I ever found them again before coming home.

For Karen, sex and rage are inextricably related. Even her anger often leads to the most violent lovemaking, in which the discharge of passion is in clear proportion to the rage that preceded it.

She once recalled her parents' violent arguments. One ended with her father's shouting at the top of his lungs, "Any whore in Pittsburgh is better in bed than you are!" To which her mother replied, "I'm glad you can get it up for the whores in Pittsburgh." There was a hidden lesson in Karen's remarks: she obviously assumes that whores free me of whatever inhibitions I still feel with her.

For those who can afford it, New York seems to have been designed as the perfect pharmacy, with remedies available around the clock, for all human ills. All except anguish. At midnight I called a neighborhood bookshop and asked the employee who answered to select twenty-five books of poetry for me and have them delivered to my hotel room. Shortly after the books arrived, Karen called and said she wasn't feeling well. She said she was probably depressed because Susan had just left to visit her ailing mother in California. I sensed Karen's need for me, but instead of inviting her over or going to see her, I told her that, if she liked, I would try to console or distract her by reading her passages from some of the well-known American poets. I said I had just had two bagfuls delivered. She hung up before I could even begin.

That left me free. To embark on a trip with yet another Strangelove from Odyssey 2001? I decided instead to do my own hunting. I went to a singles' bar and started to talk to a girl standing next to me. She was good-looking and alone, and as she watched me I could see her breasts through the thin material of her dress. She had unusually long nipples. I ordered a pitcher of sangría, and we moved to a small table and sat close together. The girl seemed self-assured, and as she observed my gestures and the way my pants hugged my thighs, I could tell that she was assessing my body. I began to think of myself as an object of desire, and the more I concentrated on her image of me, the more I desired her. I tried to imagine myself in her place and wondered if she had any idea I was doing so. I finally asked her what it was like to ponder the idea of being with a man she hardly knew. She answered that familiarity, combined with the memory of past pleasures, was for her the most potent of all aphrodisiacs; still, she said, she was able to look at a man across a room and feel that she already knew him intimately.

She asked me what I did, and I told her I lived off a rich older couple from Pittsburgh. She was horrified at first, fearing that I might be some bisexual gigolo, some human hyena scavenging among the elderly set, but I quickly dispelled her fears by inviting her for a ride in my new convertible—which, even if she assumed I had bought the car with the earnings from my unwholesome profession, she was not about to miss out on. With the top folded down, pop songs blaring on the radio and tires screeching, we drove through the empty streets of the financial district, staring up at the Wall Street skyscrapers. On the way back I stopped at the marina. The captain of my boat—whom I'd called from the bar—was waiting for me, a bit sleepy but smiling, with the boat at the ready, quietly humming, its lights on. We stepped inside, and as the captain piloted the boat down the river the girl and I had a drink on the afterdeck. By now she no longer cared how I got my money. Like a prop on a watery stage with Manhattan for a backdrop, the boat moved slowly and almost noiselessly past the Battery.

At the mouth of the Hudson we passed between two ships. The crews looked down at the three of us—a man, a woman, and a uniformed captain—looking up at them from a luxurious mini-*Titanic*.

I asked the captain to drop anchor near the Statue of Liberty, and as he sat on the flybridge watching TV, the girl and I, both naked, lay on the bed in the cabin and let the gentle roll of the boat rock us into each other's arms. At one point I was on top of her, stroking her hair, thinking, Soon I'll put it in. But something reminded me of Karen. Screwing this girl would merely have been another anecdote for Karen's amusement. Sweaty and exhausted, I turned away.

The desk clerk telephoned to say that Monsieur Bernardot was downstairs. "He says he has an appointment with you, Mr. Whalen."

"Send him up," said Whalen.

A balding, slightly stooped man in his fifties soon entered the room.

"I want you to be my cook," said Whalen, shaking his hand.

The man looked at him with reverence, then said in a heavy French accent, "My former employer, Mrs. Allcott, greatly admired your parents, sir. It was while in her service that I cooked dinner for your father and mother on several different occasions. That was shortly before you were born, Mr. Whalen. In a way," he said, smiling at the thought, "I like to think that the food I prepared on those evenings might have contributed to what a fine man you've turned out to be."

"My parents are both dead," said Whalen.

"Yes, sir, I know that. I am sorry." He paused. "Would you like to know my credentials and see my letters of reference?"

"You can leave the letters with my secretary. But tell me briefly where you've worked until now."

The man smiled. "I've worked for over thirty years in many places. I went to the Hotel School in Lyons, where I studied cooking, service, and restaurant management. I spent three years working under Paul Bocuse, possibly the greatest cook ever, and then I worked at the Beau Rivage in Lausanne and the Hotel de l'Etrier in Crans-Montana. Later I became *chef de cuisine* at the Prince Royal Hotel at Bourg-Léopold, then *chef de garde* at the Ritz in Paris. After that I had some family trouble in France and immigrated to the United States. In New York I worked first for the famous Romeo Salta, then for David Wolf, the well-known American restaurateur."

"Good," said Whalen, bored but polite.

The man went on. "The last three years I worked for Mrs. Mary Hayward Weir. I've a letter of recommendation from her. And before that I was in the employ of Mrs. Charlotte Cobb-McKay, and before—"

"Fine," Whalen interrupted. "Anything else?"

"Well, sir . . ." The man's French accent became more noticeable. "There's nothing in the field of haute cuisine that I can't do. But of course—" he paused—"of course, you can't compare what I could cook for you, let's say, in Paris, Florence, or in Crans-Montana, to what I can prepare in New York or Pittsburgh. Here, the food-freezing methods kill the flavor—"

"You are single, aren't you?" Whalen cut in.

"I am divorced. My children, all grown up, live in France."

"All right," said Whalen. "Now, as my lawyers discussed with your agency, I'm ready to pay you twice your previous salary. But you will have free time only when I am dining out or not in town. Otherwise you will have to be on call always to cook for me and my guests."

"Yes, sir," said the man. "Will I be living on the premises?"

"Yes, you will," said Whalen. "My house should be ready in a month or so. I've already hired two experienced maids, and there will be an ample cleaning staff available. That's all."

"Thank you, sir," said the man, and he bowed before leaving.

"You have asked us, Jonathan, to submit to you the findings of our screening of the applicants for the executive posts that are available from time to time in our company. These findings were obtained through the carefully monitored use of electronic Voice Stress lie detectors, sophisticated scientific testing and multidimensional personality analysis, as well as through information about each applicant's family, his professional past, his medical history, even his habits and hobbies—all acquired through our well-placed confidential sources. Eighty percent of those interviewed suffered from some disorder in the urinary tract and anal zones and admitted having sexual problems ranging from inadequate erection to complete impotence. More than forty percent complained of heart palpitation, tension, breathing difficulties, or headaches. We established that close to ninety percent of these otherwise outstanding businessmen had routinely complained about anxiety, insomnia, depression, forgetfulness, sweating, and ulcers. Your father was always in favor of such preventive screening. He called it our anti-ulcer policy. He was ahead of his time, Jonathan."

"To be really ahead of his time, my father should have trained Peruvian Indians to become his executives," I said. "According to the *Corporate Scientific*, Peruvian Indians never develop ulcers."

"Why?"

"Because they're notorious opium and cocaine smokers who lack ambition, refuse to compete, and are unwilling to plan ahead. Without tension, with no anxiety, they live only in the present—hence, they have no ulcers."

"Do you know, Jonathan, that right here in this country we have millions upon millions of lazy blacks and Hispanics with exactly that attitude? It's nice for them that we keep them all on welfare so that they can enjoy their freedom—freedom from work as well as ulcers."

In the rearview mirror Whalen saw the car following him, and he recognized his pursuers. Noting that the highway was empty except for them, he stepped on the accelerator and his car lurched forward. In a maneuver that brought back memories of his high school drives with Karen and their friends, he jerked the steering wheel to the left. As the car leaned to one side he pulled out the hand brake, locking the rear wheels, and as if lifted by a giant crane the car spun to the left, skidding and pitching. In an instant he swung the steering wheel to the right, released the hand brake, and simultaneously depressed the gas pedal. The front of the car swayed, then stabilized. Now moving in the opposite direction, he passed the pursuing car and then in the rearview mirror saw it stop suddenly. He could hear the tires squealing. Whalen sped on for about a mile, turned at an intersection, and continued speeding for another mile. Having lost his pursuers again, he slowed down, parked his car at the curb, and turned off the engine. He could hear the faint siren of a police car far away.

Whalen walked around the room glancing at the modern paintings. He paused at the window. Like an architect's scale model, Manhattan spread out below him.

"In my father's office I could open the window."

"Ah, yes," said Peter Macauley. "Those charming old-fashioned windows. Ours are all permanently sealed. Here on the hundred and sixth floor the wind is no joke." He came closer and stood next to Whalen. "Your father's office was on the twentieth floor of the dear old Coinage Building, wasn't it?"

"The twenty-fifth," said Whalen.

As Macauley returned to his office desk, he noticed Whalen looking at a panel of screens, buttons, knobs, and flickering lights on it. "Recently installed," Macauley said,

patting the desk affectionately. "Made of hand-rubbed wal-
nut. Everything is built in. This is a closed-circuit TV that
is hooked up with a videophone, so I can see those I'm on
the phone with, as long as they work for this company. I
can even freeze a single frame and create an instant portrait
of any one of them, as well as of myself." He laughed.
"And this," he said, pointing to the right, "is a conference
telephone with a hands-free speaker and an electronic touch
dial—also connected to a screen that allows me to zero in
on every participant at any conference that might be taking
place in the building—and all this from behind my desk.
Very useful. Here, farther to the right, we have a twelve-
digit memory calculator hooked into our central corporate
data bank. Every relevant business figure of our company
for the last twenty-five years is retrievable in a split second.
And here, below, special gauges compute the working time
and wear on every major piece of heavy equipment we, or
our subsidiaries, own. Don't you think, Jonathan, that your
father would have loved it?" When Whalen nodded, Macauley continued. "In only forty-five seconds this telecopier
transmits—over telephone, radio, and communication sat-
ellite—a facsimile of any document or photograph to any
part of the world. Here, above, my personal ticker tape
gives quotations of our stock and that of our affiliates. In
the center are the intercom, the Dictaphones, the paging
systems, the data-retrieval subset."

"Why isn't there equipment like that to sort out a
person's conflicting ideas and emotions?" asked Whalen.

"Well, there almost is!" exclaimed Macauley. "Pressing this little knob," he said, pointing to the desk's side,
"activates the latest polygraph—we've nicknamed it the
Nothing-but-the-Truth Machine—developed by one of our
subsidiaries. Like many other technological breakthroughs,
Nothing-but-the-Truth grew out of military intelligence research related to the interrogation of prisoners and spies.

By electronically analyzing the unconscious and involuntary stress that affects the muscles controlling the vocal cords and causes microtremor in a person's voice, this polygraph can tell when a person is telling the truth and when he is not. In addition, it alerts me to the presence of wiretaps, phone bugs, or tape recorders, either installed in my office or carried by a visitor."

"Isn't that unethical?"

"Lying and deceiving are unethical, Jonathan. Their deterrents are not.

"When your father was running the company, he was greatly in favor of introducing the latest means of increasing our efficiency. Today this company is a vast conglomerate, one of the largest in the world, with over seventy national and international subsidiaries scattered in nearly as many countries. Each year our revenues are higher than the gross national product of, say, Sweden or Spain, not to mention other less advanced countries. Our labor force, here and abroad, exceeds a million and a half men and women of different colors, speaking dozens of different languages. Metals, once your father's major preoccupation, are now only our ninth-largest interest. We are, I'm happy to say, among a handful of large corporations that, through their investments, control at least fifteen percent of the stock of the top forty conglomerates. We and the companies we own are involved in aerospace, pharmaceuticals, computers, food, coal mining, hotel chains, gas turbines, oceangoing tankers, offshore drilling, television, semiconductors, insurance, realty development, publishing, and several other industries—from prostaglandins to prefabricated housing." Reassured by Whalen's silence, he went on. "Our policies have also changed since your father's time. Although he opposed any substantial foreign acquisition of our stock, we've embarked on a different course. The West Germans, as well as Arab investors from Kuwait and the Emirates, own slightly over four percent of our equity. However, since the U.S. Securities and Exchange Commission requires full disclosure of ownership only when five percent or more of a company's stock is owned by one investor, we are within our rights to hide the identities of our foreign investors—as well as to shield from our government and the public the actual size and nature of their formidable holdings. I might add that all our foreign investors are proud to know that, without some of the products manufactured by our company, American astronauts might never have walked on the moon." Grinning, he looked at Whalen.

"So much for the myth that corporate America is owned and controlled by millions of little investors and shareholders," said Whalen, "a myth my father once fostered among his workers in Whalenburg."

"Well, you are the largest individual holder of shares in this vast enterprise—and living evidence of the fallacy of that myth, Jonathan. The House Banking Subcommittee on Domestic Finance states that ownership of from five to ten percent of a corporation's stock means 'actual control' of that corporation; that ownership of as little as one or two percent already gives the shareholder 'tremendous influence.' Now, in light of these figures, think of your own holdings."

"I do," said Whalen, "and I'm impressed by them."

"But do be seated, Jonathan," said Macauley. "Tell me what brings you all the way up here?"

Whalen sat down and stared at Macauley, who remained leaning against his desk.

"Wherever I go," said Whalen calmly, "I'm being followed, around the clock, by several men. They carry the latest walkie-talkies and they drive big sedans."

Macauley's expression did not alter. "How do you know that?" he asked.

"I've seen them. I managed to lose them once or twice,

but they always come back. They're probably downstairs waiting for me."

"Why are you telling me about it?"

"Because whatever happens to me might in some way affect this company." He paused. "It might also, however remotely, bear on your position, Mr. Macauley."

"Pete, Jonathan, Pete."

"Well, Pete, do you, by chance, know why I'm being tailed?"

Macauley looked at him. "I'll be honest with you, Jonathan. Ever since you returned to America, you've been followed—I should say protected—because it was deemed necessary by Walter Howmet, who is the company's chairman of the board."

"Does my owning a chunk of shares give Mr. Howmet the right to have me followed—for whatever reason?"

"You're the inheritor of your family's vast holdings in this company—"

"I didn't ask to be protected," Whalen interrupted.

"Walter Howmet is also your former trustee, and godfather."

"Mr. Howmet's trusteeship has ended; and he is neither my god nor my father. Why wasn't I asked? Why wasn't I told?"

"Good question. I'll take the responsibility for that. We were afraid you would be frightened if you knew. Before you arrived we didn't know much about you, and Walter, as well as other trustees, had always felt that your conduct was, shall we say, unpredictable. Apparently, while you were abroad, you came quite close to death."

"My father was drowned, so to speak, by his lovemaking. My mother may have committed suicide. Death has an investment in Whalens—or is it the other way around?"

"Don't be bitter, Jonathan. You were out of the country

for so long that we assumed you would find New York, as well as Pittsburgh, quite alien. Look what happened to you in Whalenburg. Even though the amount of your inheritance has never been made public, there is always the danger of someone going after you. We have very good reason to fear for your personal safety. Mind you, the company has absorbed the cost of this protection and will continue to absorb it."

"You are wasting the company's money," said Whalen. "Are you also recording my conversations? Videotaping my girl friends? Giving me Nothing-but-the-Truth treatment?"

Macauley laughed loudly. "These days, even the New York tabloids report your adventures with your girl friends— and I compliment you on your taste. In any case, Jonathan, all we care about is you."

Macauley opened a cabinet behind him, revealing a row of gold-topped crystal decanters. "A drink?" he offered. Whalen shook his head in refusal, and Macauley poured himself a tall Scotch. "If something should happen to you— and it could if you weren't protected—it would affect us all. This company doesn't like such risks." He sipped his drink. "Not all the wars, the terrorists, and the violence are in other countries," said Macauley. "America is no longer a safe country. Down there," Macauley pointed toward the windows, "for a small fee, hoods are willing to bludgeon a man to death. There are unscrupulous women capable of blackmailing you, creating a scandal. Given who you are, Jonathan, you're a perfect prey."

"I don't want your protection anymore. I'll hire my own bodyguard to protect myself against anyone who violates my rights."

Macauley stiffened. "As you wish, Jonathan. But if I, or this company, can be of any help, please let me know."

"Thank you, I will." Whalen got up.

Macauley escorted him to the door. "The Howmets are

eager to see you, Jonathan," he said as he shook Whalen's hand. "Have they managed to contact you yet?"

"Yes, I'm seeing them tomorrow," said Whalen.

In the outer office a woman accosted him. Young and shapely in a waist-nipping dress, she would assuredly have gotten high tips from a stint with the 2001 Love Odyssey. She looked at him with the adulation usually reserved for TV idols. "Mr. Whalen? I'm Claudia Parker, Mr. Macauley's secretary," she breathed. "I've been assigned to assist you. How about starting with a guided tour of our offices?"

"To those of us who knew and loved her, your mother's unwarranted death came as a terrible shock. Even though Walter and I were not so fortunate as to be among her intimate friends—she did not have many, you know—we'll always remember"—Mrs. Howmet paused—"the twinkle in her eye, her quiet laughter, her refinement. Your mother, Jonathan, was so deep—so sincere! Whenever I was with her, she taught me to appreciate the finer things in life." Mrs. Howmet sipped her tea and rang for a servant. "But let's talk of the living: are you still with that beautiful model?" she asked, leaning toward him.

"Karen," said Whalen, pouring himself more tea. "Yes, I am. From time to time, that is."

Mrs. Howmet did not seem to register his remark. "Walter and I keep seeing her pictures in the magazines— a ravishing girl—but Jonathan, aren't you somewhat uneasy about Karen's occupation? Hardly a day passes without reports of some model dying from drug abuse, becoming an accomplice in a crime, or blackmailing a rich lover. Why, only yesterday the TV news reported that one of them was shot to death by her jealous manager, who then took his own life. And your other friend—the one who ran off with you to London—isn't she an actress? Modeling, acting—most unstable professions!"

"Mrs. Howmet—"

"Helen," she beamed. "I held you when you were a baby. Just Helen."

"Helen, actresses and fashion models are no less stable than corporate executives, most of whom, as you know, drink excessively and suffer from anxiety, insomnia, tension, hemorrhoids, ulcers, and sexual impotence."

Hiding her discomfort, Mrs. Howmet stared at him without expression. Then, studying his face, she pleaded, "But I hope you don't plan to marry Karen—at least not yet."

"I don't want to talk about my plans," said Whalen abruptly. "Have you ever been to the Bowery?" he asked.

"The Bowery? Where is it?"

"In downtown New York. Not too far from Wall Street."

"No, Jonathan. Suburbia has its rewards, and these days I seldom drive to the city."

"Well, thousands of derelicts live in the slums of the Bowery. I thought that our company, which owns most of the Bowery real estate, might try to help them—maybe give them a decent place to live or build them a hospital or a drug rehabilitation center."

A maid brought fresh tea. Mrs. Howmet was listening attentively to Whalen.

"Go on, Jonathan."

"After all," said Whalen, "these bums, these addicts, are part of our life. We could turn the Bowery into a halfway decent place for human beings."

"But Jonathan, the company can't arbitrarily interfere in other people's lives," said Mrs. Howmet. "Its aim has never been to force others to do what they don't want to do."

"The Bowery derelicts don't know what to do," said Whalen. "They starve. They're diseased. Their sores don't heal anymore. In the Middle Ages they would have been given shelter. Today, day and night, they rot on the streets and eat out of garbage cans; they are run over by cars or beaten to death by hoods."

"Have you thought of helping them out yourself?" said Mrs. Howmet.

"I have, but that would be just another one-time hand-out, while right now, even as we sit here and talk, the company's own philanthropic foundation is spending millions of dollars sponsoring the American Soul Society, a bunch of psychic Svengalis who claim that they can provide scientific proof of the existence of the human soul—that they might even film or photograph it as it leaves the body—and the room—of a dying person!"

Mrs. Howmet leaned toward him again and gently touched his hand. "I haven't seen you for many years, Jonathan, but I've always felt you were the child Walter and I never had, so I think I can be frank. You have traveled a lot, and owing to your own painful past you are easily influenced. The company your father founded now belongs to a great number of shareholders, decent men and women who have worked throughout their lives. We are all conscious of human misery, and it has always been the company's policy, just as it was your father's, to help those who want to help themselves. Providing indisputable evidence—such as photographs or film—of man's immortal soul could be of vital interest to the entire human race. Giving money to a group of hopeless derelicts benefits no one, not even the derelicts themselves. With or without money, they'll go on satisfying their diseased appetites, drinking, taking dope, and stealing."

"But many of those derelicts want to work, to be useful," Whalen insisted. "Whenever a car stops for a red light in the Bowery, they stagger over to wipe off a windshield or to clean the side mirror. . . . If Walter and I could convince the board that because the company owns much of the Bowery real estate it is also responsible for what happens there—"

"You're talking like a character in a musical comedy, Jonathan. What would your father have said to all this?" Her voice became somber. "Don't even discuss it with Walter; he says that welfare has been our illfare, the curse of this country, that most of our federal budget goes to loafers and freeloaders and unwed mothers—"

"Walter is wrong," interrupted Jonathan. "Forty percent of the budget goes to the military, only two percent to welfare. Of the people on welfare, over half are children, a fourth are old-age recipients, and a fifth are mothers, not to mention the blind and the totally disabled."

Mrs. Howmet eyed him with deliberation. "Don't you think the company would have taken care of those derelicts ages ago if it were the right thing to do? But to take care of them would be to reward vice, to subsidize moral decay and corruption. It's not right, Jonathan, not right at all!"

Whalen got up, and Helen Howmet, putting her hand on his arm, walked him around the room. Her voice was almost a whisper now. "Walter wants to talk to you about joining the Masonic Order he belongs to. Your father belonged to it too. Walter will tell you everything you need to know. All I want to say is that it is important for you to join—important for the Order, for you, for all of us." She paused and smiled. "Oh, yes, a minor point. I think you ought to get a good haircut and some nice-fitting clothes. After all, you're settled now." She stopped and listened to a sound coming from outside. "That must be Walter now. He's very anxious to talk to you."

After the fitting, my tailor began talking about the movie and TV stars he'd dressed. His staff had gone home, and we were alone in his shop. He brought in some additional fabric samples, and then he suggested that the two of us watch an all-male porno film. I agreed. For some reason the film was upside down, and he said he didn't dare to rewind it for fear of damaging it, so we sat there watching an upside-down stag movie. Then he propositioned me. I turned him down, not only because I knew he was a phony who would probably jerk himself off and then lie to his customers about how good I was in bed, but because what upsets me about fags is their affectations, their exaggerated preoccupation with looks and manners, or the fact their need for love is narrowed down to elemental sex, its incompleteness camouflaged by theatrics. Mumbling some story about another appointment, I said I had to leave. The tailor didn't argue, and while he finished writing up my measurements he joked and gossiped about sleeping with some of the most prominent businessmen in town.

"I'm pleased to make your acquaintance, Mr. Whalen, because I've heard so much about your family. As you can tell from my job application, I've been a professional body-guard for fifteen years, ever since, at the age of twenty-two, I quit Stunts Unlimited in Hollywood. I've worked for businessmen, movie stars, television people, politicians, and foreign leaders living here in exile. What my application won't tell you, Mr. Whalen, is that I've saved the lives of several of my clients, and many have thanked me for it in writing. But to tell the truth, in two instances, I failed. One of my clients, as we worked our way through an all-black-tie crowd at the opening of a London play, was given a deadly chemical by a quick fine-needle injection right through his clothes. He slid to the floor twitching and shaking, and when he expired a few hours later everyone, including myself, thought he had had a heart attack. An autopsy revealed the true cause of death—but we still don't know who injected him.

"The other client and I were walking from his Houston office to his car, which was parked at the curb in front of the building. When I saw him fall dead, blood gushing from his chest, I assumed that his killer had fired a high-powered telescopic rifle from one of the windows or the roof of the office building across the street, and that's where I told the police to look for clues. When they found none, I began to suspect I'd given them a wrong lead. The killer was a good shot, no doubt about it, but I'm sure now that he fired an ordinary—maybe not even telescopic—rifle right up close to us. Where was he? I've figured it out. As my client and I were about to step out from the office building, I left first and looked around. When I saw no one near us on the sidewalk, no one suspicious across the street, and the traffic moving along smoothly and quite fast, I gave my client a signal that all was clear. We both ran for the car, but midway my client fell. Now, the only way my client could have been hit was if the killer was inside the closed trunk of a car, aiming and firing through a hole large enough to accommodate the barrel of his rifle and its silencer.

"In this business, Mr. Whalen, you can't trust anyone, not even yourself. Let me give you an example: my own case. Recently I was unemployed and free to please no one but myself. One afternoon I spotted this great-looking girl and followed her from Tiffany's to Carnegie Hall. I politely introduced myself and told her that I felt lonely and unwanted. When I offered to treat her to a drink, a dinner, a show, or all three, she agreed. She was about twenty, a Persian, studying languages here. We had a good evening on the town. Bright like a firebug, she was a pleasure to watch and to listen to. I tell you, Mr. Whalen, I could have fallen in love with her easily.

"Next day she came to my apartment for dinner; afterward, I planned to drive her to my rented beach shack on Long Island, where we could spend the weekend. We were in the middle of dinner when I got a phone call from a former client who wanted to talk to me about some unfinished business. I had to leave the girl, but I asked her to wait there for me—to read a book, watch TV, or do what she pleased.

"Two hours later, I hurried home and she was gone; she left me a nasty note accusing me of leaving her for a quickie with another woman. Upset, I drove to the beach anyhow, vowing not to call her anymore.

"But I liked her, so I changed my mind, and as if nothing had happened between us, I telephoned her. She sounded friendly, as though she had forgotten the incident, and she agreed to have another dinner with me.

She came on time, looking terrific, ready for the evening. This time, to give me more time to entertain her, I had one of the better restaurants deliver a fancy dinner to my apartment. During the meal, after a few glasses of good wine, she was a bit giggly, and as I watched her I got a bit overexcited myself. When she stood up after dinner, perfect in a well-fitting dress, I couldn't stand it any longer, and I put my hands over her ass. Well, that sobered her up. She slapped me and pushed me away—too hard, I must say, for my taste. I pulled back, saying nothing, and I picked up

a big Carnal Classified, a photographic listing of provoc-
atively posed female and male models, nightclub escorts,
masseuses and masseurs, and just plain any-sex whores—
all available for hire. Whenever a client of mine has asked
me to provide a girl or boy for him to go out with, I've
used Carnal Classified—as a sex-stunt casting directory,
you might say. And since I've had to accompany the client
on his date anyhow, I've often taken it upon myself to
recommend someone I have already checked out. In any
case, I threw the book in the face of my empress, then
grabbed her by the neck and forced her nose into the pictures
of all those whores. 'What makes you think, cunt, that
you're better than any of these cocksucking alley cats?' I
asked her. I was about to give her more of a hard time,
maybe even hit her, but as I said, I liked the kid, and so
I did nothing.

"After she looked through the album and calmly put
it aside, she got up and went to the bathroom. I turned on
the television and, ready to apologize, waited for her to
come out. But she seemed to be taking a long time, so I
went to the bathroom door and listened. There wasn't a
sound. I called her name; no answer. I tried to get in, but
the bitch had locked the door from inside, and when I
ordered her to open it, there was nothing doing. I called
her again; no go. When I forced the lock with a screwdriver
and got in, there was my Persian cat sprawled all naked on
the floor, her arms hanging over the edge of the bathtub,
the bathtub full of steaming hot water that was red with her
blood. My straight razor lay on the floor beside her.

"I pulled her away from the tub and laid her on the
floor. The blood still trickled out of her veins and oozed
out of the lips of the gashes in her white skin.

"Then I panicked.

"I used to date a medical student who was an intern
in a Bronx hospital, so I called her, praying to God she was

still working there. Well, she was. 'Norma,' I said, 'I have a naked kid in my flat who's cut her wrists and lost a lot of blood. What do I do?' 'Is she still breathing?' asked Norma. 'She is.' 'Bandage her wrists tightly to stop the bleeding, wrap her in a blanket, and get her here as soon as you can.' 'What if the kid dies on me on the way?' I asked. 'Then she's all yours,' said Norma. 'Don't bring her here. This is a hospital, not a morgue.'

"As I started to dress the girl, her body limp like that of a sick child, I kept asking myself what I would do if she died. Call an ambulance? That would also mean police and press. And what would I tell them? That after a nice dinner with me my date got herself naked and then, for the fun of it, went to my bathroom to kill herself? A likely story! The law wouldn't think twice before charging me with her murder. Could I risk carrying her body out in a trunk and dropping it into the river? Or should I cut her up and burn the pieces, one by one, in my self-cleaning microwave oven? That was one female anatomy lesson I didn't need!

"I carried the girl down to my car—the garage attendant winking and making some comment about my fucking a drunk—and I drove through town, praying all the way. At the hospital, Norma was waiting with a Korean intern she had picked because he knew nothing concerning what our laws said about attempted suicide. The girl was still alive, and while the intern sewed up her wrists and gave her a transfusion, Norma made sure everything was kept hushed up. In a day or two my Persian date was out of the hospital. When I asked her why she had cut her wrists, she simply said she did it to punish me.

"Now, Mr. Whalen, what if your girl decides one day to punish you like that? If she does, let's just hope you have me on your side. You see, as your bodyguard it is my duty to know all kinds of people who can be of help when you need them. As for me, I don't even mind lighting your cigarettes and giving you a good haircut.

"Of course, to protect you well, I'd have to be with you around the clock. Once I started working for you, I'd know a lot about you and your life. That's why I could conceivably be the one person most likely to sell you out. I'm telling you this not only because I want you to pay me well for the job, but because sooner or later you would've thought of the same thing anyway."

My mother had met Karen several times. After the first meeting, all my mother had to say about her was "What a pretty girl. Just lovely to look at!" Another time my mother sniffed Karen's perfume in my room and said, "Tell your little friend not to compete with skunks." The perfume was a gift from me.

Once, after a long conversation between Karen and my mother, I asked my mother what Karen had had to say to her. "Say?" exclaimed my mother. "Surely you agree, Jonathan, one doesn't listen to Karen; one just enjoys her looks!"

When I showed my mother a photograph of Karen leaning against me in the courtyard at Yale, my mother looked at it carefully and then remarked that I looked handsome but that the hedges needed trimming.

An unexpected postscript to my London psychodrama: at a party, making my way through the crowded room in search of a toilet, I felt a woman's hand on my arm. I turned around and faced Louise Hunter. She was as glamorous as I remembered her but, somehow, less radiant.

"You've never let me know if our trip made your girl friend jealous," she said, her smile an easy invitation.

"I didn't want to bother you," I said, at a loss for words. "I heard—I was told that you and Frank—"

"Oh, yes, we're divorced," she said. "Frank used my London escapade with you as proof of adultery."

"But the two of you had discussed the London trip long before we left," I said. "You told me that Frank knew the truth!"

"Frank was not after the truth." She frowned. "He was after a divorce. What's more, all that publicity about you and me did not go down well with my producers, so I wasn't given the role in the movie version of *The Financier*."

"I'm so sorry, Louise," I said, at a loss again. "I wish I could be of help."

She pulled a cigarette from her purse, and as I held out a light, her hand touched mine. "You can be, Jonathan. I'm without a job. I'll gladly play any role you can think of. In life or on the stage."

"I'm finished with psychodrama—and with pretending," I said.

"So am I. That's why I now regret I didn't let you sleep with me in London. How about making your girl friend jealous again?" she said, putting her arm through mine. "Only for real this time."

The auditorium grew silent. The lights dimmed. The all-male audience sat motionless, its gaze fixed on the bright spotlight that followed the frail old man walking slowly toward the marble podium. No one moved. Whalen was acutely aware that he had allowed himself to get caught in an irreversible process.

The secretary of the Order stumbled on one of the steps leading to the podium, but he promptly recovered his balance. He caught his breath and then in a trembling voice intoned the following statement: "Every association of men sets for itself goals which its members hope to attain through the strength of their mutual fellowship. We declare the following to be the aims of this Order: to foster the high ideals of manly character and achievement, to improve our character through intellectual pursuits, and to unite ourselves in lasting friendship and loyalty.

"But in our striving we must not forget that the individual comes first, along with his virtues: honorable ambition, fair speech, pure thoughts, and straightforward action.

"You, Jonathan James Whalen, are to be initiated into this Order, whose goals have just been declared. It is because the Brothers have thought you worthy of our trust that we have brought you into our fellowship. We invite you to share our privileges, we offer you our friendship and our loyal help in all your endeavors. We believe you are in sympathy with the goals of the Brotherhood and are prepared to make them your own. If we have erred, and if you find in our goals that which is incompatible with your own highest ideals, it is your obligation here and now to declare it."

The spotlight left the stage and settled on Whalen. The entire audience turned toward him. Trapped by their stare, rigid and mute, he summoned the memory of Barbara's funeral in Rangoon and certain words of the minister: "Of all living creatures, only the human being carries in himself the ultimate threat to his vital existence: the freedom to say yes or no to it, to reaffirm or to transcend the boundaries set for us by the indifferent world."

When Whalen said nothing, the secretary continued.

"Jonathan James Whalen, you will now rise, turn to face the Brothers, and declare your solemn assent to our purposes."

The lights in the room brightened. Whalen rose and heard his voice reciting. "I promise and make covenant with the Brothers of this Order, present and absent, to obey the constitution, traditions, and bylaws of this Order and to forward in every way within my power the goals for which it exists. So help me God."

Soon after that Whalen was sure that the time had come for him to forge his own covenant. Up to then he had felt the necessity of belonging to a place assigned to him at birth by nature and society. Suddenly the place belonged to him. And where formerly he had had to trust the knowledge and judgment of others, suddenly he felt ripe in his own knowledge of who he was and clear in his own judgment of what he had to do.

My dear Walter, my dear Helen:

As my godparents, and as the people closest to the memories of my past, you have been generous in assuming the place of moral guardianship that was left vacant by my parents. To show my gratefulness for your role in my life, I would like to invite you to be my guests on a trip abroad. Such a trip would allow me, possibly for the first time, to discover myself.

It will be a leisurely vacation trip. I've chartered a jet to take the three of us to East Africa, a region that once made a great impression on me, and I've arranged for us to live at a villa on the Indian Ocean.

At this time of year the climate in the region is very mild. We could leave any day that would be convenient for you. I do hope you will accept.

Love, and much thought,

Jonathan

Breakfast was served on the terrace overlooking the ocean. Whalen handed the binoculars to Walter Howmet. "And that's a baobab," he said, pointing at the largest tree in the garden. "*Baobab* means 'thousand-year-old,' and many people in Africa believe that the tree was the root of life and witness to the birth of the first man. The native calls the baobab 'the devil tree' because he claims that the devil once got tangled in its branches and punished the tree by reversing it. To the native, the roots are branches now, and the branches are roots. To ensure that there would be no more baobabs, the devil destroyed all the young ones. And that's why, the native says, there are only full-grown baobab trees left."

Whalen turned toward the ocean. "Look at the reef," he said. "Stretching out for miles, it's a natural barrier that protects the shallows from sharks. The reef is full of caves— each cave an aquarium, containing some of nature's most exotic creatures."

"It was so thoughtful of you, Jonathan, to bring us all the way to Africa," said Howmet, gently tapping the shell of his egg with a knife. "At our age Helen and I would never have made such a trip on our own; we would have died without ever seeing this natural paradise, wouldn't we, Helen?"

Mrs. Howmet was animated. "I just can't believe it! Only the day before yesterday we were in Woodbury, Connecticut! Look where we are now!" She took the binoculars from her husband and scanned the gleaming shallows directly before them.

"I visited here once before," Whalen said, "to watch the Aga Khan race his sand yachts on Bahati Beach. I learned how to sand-sail here."

After breakfast Whalen told the servants that he would be spending the day exploring the shallows and that he and his guests would lunch on one of the sandbars near the reef. He ordered the servants to prepare the rubber dinghy, his scuba equipment, and sandwiches, drinks, and fruits.

He checked the tide table for the time when the rising tide would flow over the reef and flood the shallows, and from the balcony of his room he watched the Howmets as they walked slowly through the villa's exotic gardens on their way to the beach. Quickly he went down and caught up with them just as they were about to board the dinghy. While the black servant and Walter steadied the small boat, Whalen helped Helen into it. Whalen and Walter climbed aboard, and Whalen started the tiny engine. When the servant cast off and the boat began to move through the clear water, the Howmets peered at the seabed through the boat's Plexiglas bottom, exclaiming appreciatively each time they saw a fish. Whalen steered the boat diagonally toward the reef, and in minutes, sky, beach, and jungle fused on the horizon behind them.

Howmet started his movie camera and trained it on his wife, who waved her straw sun hat at him as she leaned out over the water.

THE DEVIL TREE

"My mother once told me," said Whalen, "that my father divided the people he had worked with into the wets and the drys. He only trusted the wets—people who perspired—because he believed that they couldn't lie to him without being betrayed by their sweat. He never trusted the drys. Yet you, Walter, were my father's closest associate, and even in this heat you don't seem to perspire at all. I know that he trusted you, of course. My mother also trusted you."

They were now far from the mainland, and they could hear the surf crashing on the other side of the reef. Whalen selected a small sandbar, pulled the boat onto the sand, and helped his passengers disembark. He and Walter removed the supplies from the boat and stretched a beach blanket out on the sand. Meanwhile Helen filmed the colorful starfish that were spread on the sand near the water's edge.

"What a sweet little island this is! A paradise in the middle of the ocean, miles from the shore, from other beaches—from anything!" Mrs. Howmet exclaimed rapturously. "Only these few starfish. And the sand looks as if it's just been washed," she marveled.

Whalen collected his underwater gear. Through his binoculars he searched the ocean for traces of a boat and scanned the faraway beach for any native dugouts. Nothing. The world was empty.

"I guess the ocean does wash over this island once in a while, particularly in a storm," Whalen said distractedly. He was listening to the surf swelling up behind the reef.

Helen filmed her husband as he helped Whalen fasten his air tanks. When everything was ready, Whalen walked into the water. He, dived toward the coral bed and swam along the sandy bottom, frightening schools of fish that zigzagged around him. In one of the coral crannies he saw a blue blowfish. Ready to defend itself, the fish puffed up, and Whalen cornered and caught it, cradling it in his hands. He emerged at the sandbar, surprising the Howmets, who were resting on the blanket with their ankles crossed, their pale faces half hidden under their hats. While Helen filmed · the blowfish, her husband took still photographs of her filming the fish.

"I'm leaving you again," said Whalen. "I want to chase sea snakes."

Walter smiled and Helen waved her hand. Then they both lay back, pulling their hats over their faces for a nap in the sun. As Whalen walked past the dinghy, he dropped the blowfish back into the sea and casually threw the boat's towrope overboard. He dived into the water, and from beneath the surface he grabbed the rope and pulled it, easing the boat slowly off its perch. Once free of the sandbar, the dinghy, pushed by the wind and tide, would aimlessly drift away. Whalen began his long swim back to the villa.

Looking back at the Howmets, two mere spots now on the patch of sand, Whalen felt abruptly severed from the whole breadth of his past. When the Howmets were no longer in sight, he felt as if he were at last able to look toward himself, to rise up and anchor himself on a sandbar of his own.

He saw a sea snake, poised to attack as it followed him, and keeping an eye on the creature he swam submerged until the sea snake left him for another target. He rose to the water's surface and looked back. As the rising tide rolled over the reef, the sandbar, like a water-skier cut from a towrope, vanished under the curling waves.

Whalen emerged on Ukunda's beach. The jungle was still, the sky cloudless, the sea tranquil. The world was in order.

Reaching the villa, he summoned the servants and instructed them to launch the speedboat and start looking for his missing guests. While he was skin-diving, he explained, the Howmets must have gone exploring in the dinghy. Now, he said, he was worried about their being out there all alone, at the mercy of the incoming tide.

The bodies of Helen and Walter Howmet were never found, and Whalen, like a starving man who had suddenly been nourished from an unknown source, felt new energy flowing into him. But there were often moments when he gave in to fatigue and a sense of futility, when he felt as though he were living on the far side of communicable thoughts and feelings. He fought these moments, trying to tear off the membrane that seemed to enclose his mind and inhibit his will. But he was helpless, beyond self-control.

He confronted himself. He could remain free, setting the rules for his own acts and determining the value of their consequences, with Karen as the intermediary through whom he would discover himself. Or he could try to perceive himself without Karen, as a man who knows himself only through principles set for him by the world.

Then he thought of the lesson taught by the Indian Panchadasi concerning the Self: "How shall I grasp it? Do not grasp it. That which remains when there is no more grasping is the Self."

Dearest Jonathan:

I remember being in your room at Yale when we both read aloud and recognized ourselves in a passage from Rilke: "We discover, indeed, that we do not know our part: we look for a mirror; we want to rub off the paint, to remove all that is artificial, and to become real. But somewhere a bit of masking that we forget still clings to us. A trace of exaggeration remains in our eyebrows; we do not notice that the corners of our lips are twisted. And thus we go about, a laughingstock, a mere half-thing: neither real beings nor actors." But now with you, I'm not a laughingstock, a mere half-thing. I'm as real as are my emotions, and of all people I know and care for, you're the closest to me.

When I was a girl, I thought that loving was magic—magic that made one's lover free, happy, fruitful, fulfilled. I've fastened all my desires on you because you're my pleasure, my freedom, my occasion for joy. Fastening on you has given me a new gravity—the dependable force of our love. Now, free to do anything, go anywhere, be with anyone, I'm secure in the knowledge that our love will always bring me back to you. The loss of you would be a wound for which I have no balm.

Karen

Karen undid the top button of her blouse and with a single movement crossed her arms and lifted the thin fabric over her head. Her breasts quivered as she shifted her body to unzip her skirt and slide it over her hips. Still looking at him, she hooked her thumbs in the waistband of her black slip and pushed it very slowly down to her ankles. Then she stepped away from the small pile of clothing.

She bowed her head, lay down on the rug, and spread her hands. Her calves tensed as she thrust out her toes. He stared at the mirror that was propped against the wall and saw himself slip into her. Soon, her skin dry and cool against him, he could not distinguish between her flesh and his own. He probed deeper. Her face glistened in the light, and as she spread her thighs wide she drew her fingers together behind his back.

Still fixed on their reflection in the mirror, he saw himself and Karen doubled up, clutching each other, thrusting, the mirror a witness of the last moment of his intoxication, of his useless passion. He looked away, then withdrew. He stood up.

He pulled her up by the arm and sat her on the chair. As he held her by the shoulder with one hand, he brought the open palm of his other hand down on her face. She recoiled; he held her fast and, his hand a fist now, struck her once again. She spun away, gasping, and he let her fall into the chair facedown. No longer could he see her eyes.

Karen remained motionless. He waited for her to scream or try to hit him, but she did not. Without looking at her, he walked across the room, opened the door to his study, entered, and shut the door behind him.

He lay in his bed in the Swiss clinic, fully dressed, staring at the ceiling. In pain but not knowing why, he only wanted his mind turned off. The simplest tasks—dressing or undressing, turning the light on or off, closing or opening the window—seemed beyond his will and strength.

He could sense the coming of day without opening his eyes, even when the shutters of his room were closed. Awake long before the staff, he listened for the day's first sound: a footstep in the clinic's corridors, the rumbling of a bus through the streets, the buzz of a motorboat on Lake Geneva.

He lay like a stone on the shore, unmoved by the waves washing over him. A heavy weight seemed to press constantly against his chest.

Once in a while he longed for change, and he knew that the longing itself was a prelude to recovery. But the longing tired him, and then all he wanted was to endure. His thoughts returned to the faraway hospital in Rangoon, to the words of Abraham Joshua Heschel: "To my heart I am of great moment. The challenge I face is how to actualize, how to concretize the quiet eminence of my being."

One night Whalen's body refused to sleep. He rose, left the clinic, and walked to the shore of the lake. A sheet of mist rolled along the water, hiding all but the nearest banks from view. The smell of moss spread through the air. He sniffed the dew, listened to the lapping of the water against the stones of the lakeshore, and felt the skin prickle on the back of his neck. The fog lifted. He stared across the lake and saw the blinking lights of Geneva.

ON KOSINSKI

*Jerzy Kosinski has lived through—and now makes
use of—some of the strongest direct experience
that this century has had to offer.*

TIME

To appreciate the violent, ironic, suspenseful, morally demanding world of JERZY KOSINSKI's novels, one must first
acknowledge the random succession of pain and joy, wealth and
poverty, persecution and approbation that have made his own life
often as eventful as those of his fictional creations.

He was born in Poland. When he was six, all but two members
of his once numerous and distinguished family were lost in the
Holocaust of World War II. Abandoned, suspected of being a Jew
or a gypsy, he fled alone from village to village in Nazi-occupied
eastern Europe, working as a farm hand, gaining his knowledge
of nature, animal life, farming—and survival. At the age of nine,
in a traumatic confrontation with a hostile peasant crowd he lost
the power of speech, and was unable to talk for over five years.
After the war, he was reunited with his ailing parents (his father
was a scholar of ancient linguistics, his mother a pianist) and
placed in a school for the handicapped. While on vacation, he
regained his voice in a skiing accident, and with renewed self-
reliance promptly worked his way through high school.

During his studies at the state-controlled Stalinist college and
university he was suspended twice and often threatened with ex-
pulsion for his rejection of the official Marxist doctrine. While
a Ph.D candidate in social psychology, he rose rapidly to become

an associate professor and grantee of the Academy of Sciences, the state's highest research institution. Attempting to free himself from state-imposed collectivity, he would spend winters as a ski instructor in the Tatra Mountains, and summers as a social counselor at a Baltic sea resort.

Meanwhile, secretly, he plotted his escape. A confident master of bureaucratic judo, Kosinski pitted himself against the Establishment. In need of official sponsors, and reluctant to implicate his family, his friends and the academy staff, he created four distinguished—but fictitious—members of the Academy of Sciences to act in that capacity. As a member of the Academy's inner circle and a prize-winning photographer (with many one-man exhibitions to his credit), Kosinski had access to state printing plants, and he was able to furnish each academician with the appropriate official seals, rubber stamps and stationery. His punishment, had he been caught, would have been many years in prison. After two years of active correspondence between his fictitious sponsors and the various government agencies, Kosinski obtained an official passport allowing him to visit the United States under the auspices of an equally fictitious American "foundation." Waiting for his U.S. visa, expecting to be arrested at any time, Kosinski carried a foil-wrapped egg of cyanide in his pocket. "One way or another," he vowed, "they won't be able to keep me here against my will." But his plan worked. On December 20, 1957, Kosinski arrived in New York fluent in several languages though only with a rudimentary knowledge of English, following what he still considers the singular most creative act of his life. "I left behind being an inner emigré trapped in spiritual exile," he says. "America was to give shelter to my real self and I wanted to become its writer-in-residence." He was twenty-four years of age—his American odyssey was about to begin.

He started wandering widely in the United States as a truck driver, moonlighting as a parking lot attendant, a cinema projectionist, a portrait photographer, a limousine and racing-car driver for a black nightclub enterpreneur. "By working in Harlem as a white, uniformed chauffeur I broke a color barrier of the profession," he recalls. Studying English whenever he could in a year he learned it well enough to obtain a Ford Foundation fellowship. Two years later, as a student of social psychology, he wrote the first of his two nonfiction books on collective society. It became an instant bestseller, serialized by *The Saturday Evening Post*, condensed by *Reader's Digest*, and published in 18 languages. He was firmly set on a writing career.

After his publishing debut he met Mary Weir, the widow of a steel magnate from Pittsburgh. They dated for two years and were married after the publication of Kosinski's second nonfiction book.

During his 10 years with Mary Weir (which ended with her death) Kosinski moved with utmost familiarity in the world of heavy industry, big business and high society. He and Mary traveled a great deal—there was a private plane, a 17-crew boat, and houses in Pittsburgh, New York, Hobe Sound, Southampton, Paris, London and Florence. He led a life most novelists only invent in the pages of their novels.

"During my marriage, I had often thought that it was Stendhal or F. Scott Fitzgerald, both preoccupied with wealth they themselves did not have, who deserved to have had my experience. At first, I considered writing a novel about my immediate American experience, the dimension of wealth, power and high society that surrounded me, not the terror, poverty and privation I had seen and experienced so shortly before. But during my marriage I was too much a part of that world to extract from it the nucleus of what I felt. As a writer, I perceived fiction as the art of imaginative projection and so, instead, I decided to write my first novel about a homeless boy in war-torn Eastern Europe, an existence I'd once led and also one that was shared by millions of others like me, yet was still foreign to most Americans. This novel, *The Painted Bird*, was my gift to Mary, and to my new world."

His following novels—*Steps, Being There, The Devil Tree, Cockpit, Blind Date* and *Passion Play*, all links in an elaborate fictional cycle, were inspired by particular events of his life. He would often draw on the experience he had gained when, once a "Don Quixote of the turnpike," he had become a "Captain Ahab of billionaire's row." "Kosinski has enough technical virtuosity to outwrite almost any competitor," wrote *Los Angeles Herald Examiner*, "but few novelists have a personal background like his to draw on." Translated into most major languages, at first his novels have earned Kosinski the status of an international underground culture hero. Official recognition followed: for *The Painted Bird*, the French Best Foreign Book Award; for *Steps*, the National Book Award. He received a Guggenheim fellowship, the Award in Literature of the American Academy and the National Institute of Arts and Letters, as well as the Brith Sholom Humanitarian Freedom Award, and many others.

While Kosinski was constantly on the move, living and writing in various parts of the United States, Europe and Latin America, close calls with death persisted in his life. On his way from Paris to the Beverly Hills home of his friend, film director Roman Polanski, and his wife, Sharon Tate, Kosinski's luggage was unloaded by mistake in New York. Unable to catch the connecting flight to Los Angeles, Kosinski reluctantly stayed overnight in New York. That very night in Polanski's household the Charles Manson Helter-Skelter gang murdered five people—among them Kosinski's closest friends, one of whom he financially assisted in leaving Europe and settling in the States.

For the next few years Kosinski taught English at Princeton and Yale. He left university life when he was elected president of American P.E.N., the international association of writers and editors. After serving the maximum two terms, he has remained active in various American human rights organizations. He is proud to have been responsible for freeing from prisons, helping financially, resettling or otherwise giving assistance to a great number of writers, political and religious dissidents and intellectuals all over the world, many of whom openly acknowledged his coming to their rescue.

Called by *America* "a spokesman for the human capacity to survive in a highly complex social system," Kosinski has been often labeled by the media an existential cowboy, a Horatio Alger of the nightmare, a penultimate gamesman, the utterly portable man and a mixture of adventurer and social reformer. In an interview for *Psychology Today*, Kosinski said: "And I have no habits that require maintaining—I don't even have a favorite menu—the only way for me to live is to be as close to other people as life allows. Not much else stimulates me—and nothing interests me more."

Traveling extensively, on an average Kosinski wakes up around 8 A.M. ready for the day. Four more hours of sleep in the afternoon allows him to remain mentally and physically active until the early dawn when he retires. This pattern, he claims, benefits his writing, his photography, and practicing of the sports he has favored for years—downhill skiing and polo, which, as an avid all-around horseman, he plays on a team—or one-on-one.

As a novelist and a screeplay writer (he adapted for the screen his novel, *Being There* which starred Peter Sellers, Shirley MacLaine, Melvyn Douglas and Jack Warden, for which he was nominated for the Golden Globe and won the Writers Guild of America Best Screenplay of the Year Award)—Kosinski is frequently interviewed by the press and appears often on television. Thus, he is apt to be recognized, and to obtain private access to public places he sometimes disguises himself; occasionally, he takes part-time employment in businesses and corporations that interest him.

A critic once said of Kosinski that he "writes his novels so sparsely as though they cost a thousand dollars a word, and a misplaced or misused locution would cost him his life." He was close to the truth: Kosinski takes almost three years to write a novel, and rewrites it a dozen times; later, in subsequence sets of proofs, he condenses the novel's text often by one-third. Kosinski said that "writing fiction is the essence of my life—whatever else I do revolves around a constant thought: could I—can I—would I—should I—use it in my next novel? As I have no children, no family, no relatives, no business or estate to speak of, my books are my only spiritual accomplishment."

"Learning from the best writing of every era—wrote *The Washington Post*—Kosinski develops his own style and technique. . . . in harmony with his need to express new things about our life and the world we do live in, to express the inexpressible. Giving to himself as well as to the reader the same chance for interpretation, he traces the truth in the deepest corners of our outdoor and indoor lives, of our outer appearance and our inner reality. He moves the borderline of writing to more remote, still invisible and untouchable poles, in cold and in darkness. Doing so, he enlarges the borders of the bearable."

BESTSELLERS FROM ARROW

All these books are available from your bookshop or newsagent or you can order them direct. Just tick the titles you want and complete the form below.

A CHOICE OF CATASTROPHIES	Isaac Asimov	£1.95
BRUACH BLEND	Lillian Beckwith	95p
THE HISTORY MAN	Malcolm Bradbury	£1.60
A LITTLE ZIT ON THE SIDE	Jasper Carrott	£1.25
EENY MEENY MINEY MOLE	Marcel A'Agneau	£1.50
HERO	Leslie Deane	£1.75
TRAVELS WITH FORTUNE	Christine Dodwell	£1.50
11th ARROW BOOK OF CROSSWORDS	Frank Henchard	95p
THE LOW CALORIE MENU BOOK	Joyce Hughes	90p
THE PALMISTRY OF LOVE	David Brandon-Jones	£1.50
DEATH DREAMS	William Katz	£1.25
PASSAGE TO MUTINY	Alexander Kent	£1.50
HEARTSOUNDS	Marth Weinman Lear	£1.75
LOOSELY ENGAGED	Christopher Matthew	£1.25
HARLOT	Margaret Pemberton	£1.60
TALES FROM A LONG ROOM	Peter Tinniswood	£1.50
INCIDENT ON ATH	E. C. Tubb	£1.15
THE SECOND LADY	Irving Wallace	£1.75
STAND BY YOUR MAN	Tammy Wynette	£1.75
DEATH ON ACCOUNT	Margaret Yorke	£1.00
	Postage	
	Total	

ARROW BOOKS, BOOKSERVICE BY POST, PO BOX 29, DOUGLAS, ISLE OF MAN, BRITISH ISLES

Please enclose a cheque or postal order made out to Arrow Books Limited for the amount due including 10p per book for postage and packing for orders within the UK and 12p for overseas orders.

Please print clearly

NAME ....

ADDRESS..

....

Whilst every effort is made to keep prices down and to keep popular books in print, Arrow Books cannot guarantee that prices will be the same as those advertised here or that the books will be available.